PRAISE FOR SECO[

"[SecondWorld] is gripping, propelled by expertly controlled pacing and lively characters. Robinson's punchy prose style will appeal to fans of Matthew Reilly's fast-paced, bigger-than-life thrillers, but this is in no way a knockoff. It's a fresh and satisfying thriller that should bring its author plenty of new fans."

— Booklist

"A brisk thriller with neatly timed action sequences, snappy dialogue and the ultimate sympathetic figure in a badly burned little girl with a fighting spirit... The Nazis are determined to have the last gruesome laugh in this efficient doomsday thriller."

— Kirkus Reviews

"Relentless pacing and numerous plot twists drive this compelling stand-alone from Robinson... Thriller fans and apocalyptic fiction aficionados alike will find this audaciously plotted novel enormously satisfying."

— Publisher's Weekly

"A harrowing, edge of your seat thriller told by a master storyteller, Jeremy Robinson's Secondworld is an amazing, globetrotting tale that will truly leave you breathless."

— Richard Doestch, bestselling author of THE THIEVES OF LEGEND

"Robinson blends myth, science and terminal velocity action like no one else."

— Scott Sigler, NY Times bestselling author of PANDEMIC

"Just when you think that 21st-century authors have come up with every possible way of destroying the world, along comes Jeremy Robinson."

— New Hampshire Magazine

PRAISE FOR THE JACK SIGLER THRILLERS

THRESHOLD

"Threshold elevates Robinson to the highest tier of over-the-top action authors and it delivers beyond the expectations even of his fans. The next Chess Team adventure cannot come fast enough."

— Booklist - Starred Review

INSTINCT

"Robinson's slam-bang second Chess Team thriller [is a] a wildly inventive yarn that reads as well on the page as it would play on a computer screen."

— Publisher's Weekly

"Intense and full of riveting plot twists, it is Robinson's best book yet, and it should secure a place for the Chess Team on the A-list of thriller fans who like the over-the-top style of James Rollins and Matthew Reilly."

— Booklist

PULSE

"Rocket-boosted action, brilliant speculation, and the recreation of a horror out of the mythologic past, all seamlessly blend into a rollercoaster ride of suspense and adventure."
— James Rollins, NY Times bestselling author of THE EYE OF GOD

"Jeremy Robinson has one wild imagination, slicing and stitching his tale together with the deft hand of a surgeon. Robinson's impressive talent is on full display in this one."

— Steve Berry, NY Times bestselling author of
THE KING'S DECEPTION

"There's nothing timid about Robinson as he drops his readers off the cliff without a parachute and somehow manages to catch us an inch or two from doom."

— Jeff Long, NY Times bestselling author of DEEPER

"An elite task force must stop a genetic force of nature in the form of the legendary Hydra in this latest Jeremy Robinson thriller. Yet another page-turner!"

— Steve Alten, NY Tmes bestselling author of
THE OMEGA PROJECT

"Robinson's latest reads like a video game with tons of action and lots of carnage. The combination of mythology, technology, and high-octane action proves irresistible."

— Booklist

GUARDIAN

A JACK SIGLER CONTINUUM NOVELLA

JEREMY ROBINSON

WITH J. KENT HOLLOWAY

BREAKNECK MEDIA

ALSO BY JEREMY ROBINSON

Standalone Novels
The Didymus Contingency
Raising The Past
Beneath
Antarktos Rising
Kronos
Xom-B (2014)

SecondWorld Novels
SecondWorld
I Am Cowboy

Kaiju Novels
Island 731
Project Nemesis
Project Maigo

The Antarktos Saga
The Last Hunter – Descent
The Last Hunter – Pursuit
The Last Hunter – Ascent
The Last Hunter – Lament
The Last Hunter – Onslaught
The Last Hunter – Collected Edition

The Jack Sigler Novels
Prime
Pulse
Instinct
Threshold
Ragnarok
Omega
Savage (2014)

The Jack Sigler Continuum Series
Guardian

The Chess Team Novellas
Callsign: King
Callsign: Queen
Callsign: Rook
Callsign: King 2 – Underworld
Callsign: Bishop
Callsign: Knight
Callsign: Deep Blue
Callsign: King 3 – Blackout

Chess Team Novella Collected Editions
Callsign: King – The Brainstorm Trilogy
Callsign – Tripleshot
Callsign – Doublshot

Writing as Jeremy Bishop
Torment
The Sentinel
The Raven
Refuge:
>*Night of the Blood Sky*
>*Darkness Falls*
>*Lost in the Echo*
>*Ashes and Dust*
>*Bonfires Burning Bright*
>*Refuge Omnibus*

ALSO BY J. KENT HOLLOWAY

The ENIGMA Directive Series
Primal Thirst
Sirens' Song
Devil's Child

The Dark Hollows Mystery Series
The Curse of One-Eyed Jack
The Dirge of Briaresnare Marsh

The Knightshade Legacy Series
The Djinn

Short Stories
"Freakshow" (An ENIGMA Directive Short Story)
"Masquerade at One Thousand Feet"
"Haunted Melody" (A Meikle Bay Horror Short Story)

GUARDIAN

A JACK SIGLER CONTINUUM NOVELLA

To all those who protect and serve.

To those who fight the good fight for the safety and security of us all.

To all those who risk everything as 'guardians' in a dangerous world.

THE CONTINUUM SERIES

Jack Sigler: A Man Out of Time

Jack Sigler was a modern soldier. First for the Army, then for the anti-terror Delta unit known as 'Chess Team' and finally for *Endgame*, a black budget organization specializing in fending off strange and otherworldly global threats. After several brutal, yet successful missions, the man known by the callsign: King, found himself torn away from his family and thrust back in time, abandoned in the year 780 BC. But that's not where his life would end. He was gifted with regenerative powers, making him nearly immortal. He heals quickly. Doesn't age. And he's nearly 2800 years away from his daughter and fiancée.

Now, the only way he can return to his own time and his family is to live, fight and sometimes wage war through the oncoming centuries, carrying on Endgame's mission: to protect the weak, right wrongs and send the world's monsters back to whatever hell spawned them.

Guardian, the first tale in the Jack Sigler Continuum series, takes place after King has lived in the past for over two hundred years...

Prologue

Mount Mashu, Zagros Mountain Range
Persia, 576 BC

Few men in all the earth were courageous enough to raise the gods of chaos, but Sereb-Meloch counted himself among those brave souls. In fact, today, the unnaturally lanky high priest intended to go one step beyond. The lesser gods were of no concern to him. Nothing but the fiercest of goddesses would be enough to accomplish what he'd planned for so long. After all, only the mother of all gods could destroy the world.

Sereb-Meloch smiled, allowing the thought to finally filter through the near-impenetrable wall of caution he'd erected over the years. His smile broadened as he placed the ancient ceremonial headdress of his goddess on his head. He stepped from his tent and out into the crisp, frigid air hanging over the summit of fabled Mount Mashu, on the outer edge of the Fertile Crescent. He gazed out at the orange-red glow of the sun as it began to slide just under the horizon. The near-blinding snow blanketing the earth, and the grand cedar trees surrounding them, gradually transformed into unsettling shades of purple and blue.

Despite the setting sun, however, his band of nearly one-hundred and forty slaves still chipped away at the rocky slope of the mountainside, in rhythm to the beat of their driver's drums. They'd been at it for nearly three weeks now and the treacherous climb to their current location, along with the hours of grueling labor to clear the rocky debris, had claimed one third of the crew.

The loss of his men mattered little. Sereb-Meloch would gladly have sacrificed ten thousand more to reach what was behind those gods-forsaken rocks, deposited by a rockslide a millennia before. The Gate of Shamash. The doorway, the legends said, used by Gilgamesh himself on his journey toward immortality. Trivialities such as eternal life mattered little to Sereb-Meloch. For him, they were the doors that would open the pathway to *Her*, and thus, to power beyond anyone's ability to imagine.

For centuries, scholars and adventurers erroneously had believed the gate lay somewhere within the lush mountains of Lebanon. Years of careful study had proven those theories false. It was only through years of patient research and the will of his most faithful goddess that the true location along the eastern border of Persia, on the edge of the Zagros mountain range, had been revealed to the priest.

"Ba'al Sereb-Meloch! Ba'al!" cried one of his priests, drawing him from his reverie. He looked over to the man called Jereziah, fur-covered robes wafting behind him as he raced up to the priest, wheezing for breath. "We have broken through!"

The high priest turned his lean frame toward the rocky debris and smiled. "Excellent. And Shamash's Gate?"

Jereziah nodded. "Exposed. But it will take a while longer to be able to fully open them."

"How much longer?"

"Another twelve hours, at least."

Sereb-Meloch glanced at the sky. Dusk was quickly slipping into night. In twelve hours, the sun would be creeping once more over the horizon, and it would be too late. They would once more have to wait for the sun to set, before they could open the gate, and that was one more wasted day for which he had no patience.

"That is not good enough," he said. "Work the slaves harder. The Gate must be open by midnight, if we are to retrieve our prizes before the rising sun."

"But your grace..."

"See that it is done, Jereziah."

The neophyte priest frowned, but nodded his understanding and scurried off, already shouting to rouse the workers. The sound of the whip intensified, and the drivers' voices raged against their charges. He allowed himself a few minutes to watch the renewed vigor with which the arduous work was done, then he gestured to the mercenary captain, Zaidu, who was currently keeping watch at the doorway to a nondescript tent in the center of the camp. When the captain approached, Sereb-Meloch returned his salute, then spoke.

"How is our guest doing this evening?" he asked.

"Beastly, that one," Zaidu growled as he tilted his head to indicate the tent. "I will be glad when he is dead. He bit my arm again this morning. Gave him a bloody nose in exchange for it. I doubt he will give us any more problems."

Sereb-Meloch regarded the captain coolly. The prisoner was not to be harmed. At all. But the mercenary scum he'd hired apparently hadn't taken him seriously. Nor did any of them remotely show the proper respect due to a man of his stature. Issues that would undoubtedly be rectified soon, but for now, he would maintain a modicum of civility toward the soldiers-for-hire in his employ. Soon enough, when the gates were finally open, he'd have no more use for any of them. What lay inside, coupled with his own band of warrior-priests, would be more than enough to liberate *Her*. The mercenaries, he decided, would be a welcome diversion for those that had slumbered for so long within the mountain. In the meantime, he'd tolerate the mongrel's barbarous behavior.

"Fine, fine," he said, grinding his teeth with each word. "But it is almost time. Assist the priests as they prepare him for the Gate's opening. Bring him to the stone and secure him to it. When the Gate is finally opened, he will be the first thing they will see."

"And who is it that lives beyond those gates? You have yet to tell us what it is we are after. All we have had to go on is rumor and the tales of old wives."

Sereb-Meloch willed his eyes not to involuntarily roll in annoyance at the impertinent question. These mercenaries had no concept of their proper place. The sooner these simpletons were dead, the better.

"Namtar and Tiamba," the high priest offered.

The mercenary stared blankly. "Who?"

"It matters not. You will see for yourself, soon enough." Sereb-Meloch paused, allowing his wolfish grin to soften a bit. "And you will witness their terrible might firsthand...as they lay claim to our sacrifice."

Zaidu scowled, obviously uneasy with that last part. An irony, really, considering the fact that he would undoubtedly kill his own mother, were the pay good enough. Strangely, the sacrifice of their prisoner, who had been nothing but a nuisance since they'd captured him, caused a moral dilemma for the black-hearted soldier.

Interesting, Sereb-Meloch thought.

"Do we have an understanding here?" he asked, forcing the captain to look him in the eye.

The mercenary nodded. "I will get the foreigner, Achelous, to help us. He has been effective with the prisoner. Has a way of calming him down."

"Fine. Fine," Sereb-Meloch repeated, waving the man off with disinterest. He didn't care how it was done. His only concern was that the prisoner be bound to the sacrificial stone before the gate was opened. Before Zaidu reached the prisoner's tent, Sereb-Meloch turned away, focusing once more on his laborers, as they pressed forward into the widening gap. *At their current pace, they might finish on time.* In the meantime, all he could do was wait and watch the work unfold.

Hours later, Sereb-Meloch clapped twice, signaling his men to bring out the prisoner. The handful of mercenaries scrambled to comply, rushing around to the opening of the tent and pulling back the door flaps. The tall, fairer skinned warrior—Zaidu had called him Achelous—stepped inside and disappeared from view. A minute later, he reemerged with a young, struggling boy in tow.

The boy—called Belshazzar—was the future heir to the Babylonian empire. He let out a string of curses on the men, as he was lifted off the ground by three of them and carried toward the stone slab. Sereb-Meloch watched in amuse-ment as the whelp—he was no more than twelve years old—kicked one of the guards in the side of the head, eliciting a howl of pain and no small amount of blood.

The boy has great power, the high priest thought, reflecting on the man's head wound. *Good. It will make the sacrifice all the sweeter.*

The battle-hardened warriors struggled to carry the squirming prince down the mud-covered slope to the altar, then roughly dropped him on the slab before securing him with leather straps, at his wrists and ankles. The prince screamed, promising vengeance on all who had abused him, as he tugged futilely at his bonds.

"Your highness," Sereb-Meloch said as he strode to the altar. "Please do not struggle. You might injure yourself."

Belshazzar growled at the high priest. His eyes narrowed with murderous hatred toward his captor. "Ba'al Marduk will cut the soul from your body and feast upon it for what you are doing to me, heretic! I will dance on your grave in honor of my grandfather."

Sereb-Meloch chuckled. He had not been called a heretic for nearly two decades, and to hear it now, uttered from the lips of this arrogant child, brought more joy to him than he would have imagined. Not for the words them-selves—they were a source of shame for him, after all—but because the beliefs he'd heralded for so long, the same beliefs that had labeled him as such, were about to be proven true. He was about to succeed in the lifelong quest that had seen him banished by the prince's grandfather, Nebuchadnezzar, so many years ago.

"I doubt you will ever have the ch—" He was interrupted the shouts of a cadre of his priests running up to him.

"Ba'al, we have done it," said one of the priests. Sereb-Meloch could never recall the man's name for some reason. "We have cleared the entrance!"

The high priest turned to Jereziah, who'd been lagging behind due to his rotund girth. "Is this true?"

The fat priest nodded, excitement evident across his features.

"And the key? Did you find a place for the key?"

Another nod. "The Gate awaits you, Ba'al. With a turn of the key, your new warriors will be set free."

Sereb-Meloch looked down at the Babylonian prince, still struggling to free himself from the leather bonds. "No," he said. "Not yet. First, we must feed them."

1

The locking mechanism to Shamash's Gate squealed in protest as the ancient bronze artifact turned against the gears. The key—an artifact of unknown origin—had taken Sereb-Meloch eight years to locate and another three to retrieve. It had required a fierce battle with a particularly brutal tribe in the northern-most part of the world, one filled with men of unusual yellow-orange hair and thick, braided beards. As with his current expedition, he'd lost hundreds of men, but he'd succeeded in the end. The ignorant chieftain from the north had had no idea of the value of the strange, cylindrical object that had been passed down in his family for nearly ten generations. It was his ransom for surrender to Sereb-Meloch's more ingenious and determined forces.

A rush of air hissed from the seam of the sealed gate, after centuries of being closed to the outside world. The high priest stepped back to admire the monstrous barricade that separated him from the second part of his plan. The door itself was a marvel of ancient ingenuity. A construction that could have come only from the gods themselves. Standing nearly forty feet in the air and made of a polished metal unknown to metal smiths, it was etched with rows of strange writings arranged in a semi-circle just below the door's lintel. The words, lost forever through ages of disuse, were probably warnings of some kind, he surmised. Vague and threatening exhortations used to scare away the superstitious.

The builder would, however, find Sereb-Meloch not easily cowed.

"Open it." He glanced over at Zaidu and nodded toward the gate.

The mercenary captain's eyes widened. "What? Me?"

The high priest cast a reproving look before nodding. "You will not be able to open it by yourself, of course." He gestured around to the mercenary force milling nervously around. "Choose three of your strongest men to assist you."

"But...but..."

"Captain Zaidu, is there a problem?"

The mercenary swallowed as he turned his gaze up at the enormous metal abomination before him.

"Is this not something the slaves should do?" he asked.

The priest feigned surprise at the suggestion. "Would you trust such a noble task to the hands of a common slave?" He shook his head in disappointment. "Such a job should be handled only by the bravest and most esteemed of men. After all, it was warriors who sealed the door. It is only fitting that warriors should be the ones to open it as well."

Another hard swallow. Zaidu looked around at his men and with a nod, chose the largest three. Exhaling nervously, he then directed his chosen three to position themselves at the seam separating the gate from cliff face. Two of his men reached their hands apprehensively into the crack of the door, while the third and Zaidu himself clutched the gigantic metal ring at the center. On the count of three, each man began pulling with all their might. The metal creaked violently, but the door slid open, revealing a narrow six inch opening. A gust of putrid, stale air spewed from the opening, the stench nearly unbearable.

"Wait!" Sereb-Meloch shouted, nearly beside himself with anticipation. This was taking entirely too long. They were losing precious night. He pointed at the foreign mercenary, Achelous, a tall, burly man with a thick mane of black hair and a full beard. The man's dark eyes stared back at him with a calm uncharacteristic of the typical rabble among Zaidu's men. "You. Help them."

The man, his stern face completely unreadable to the high priest, saluted and moved over to help his brethren-at-arms. Reaching his hand into the small opening, Achelous counted quietly to three and each man once more pulled with all their might. When the door failed to budge another inch, the man stepped back a few feet, put his hands on his waist, and looked up at the door, as if thinking the problem through.

Oh, I like this one, Sereb-Meloch thought. *He is not a mindless brute like the rest of his compatriots. This one most definitely is different.*

After several seconds of contemplation, the foreigner moved over to the garrison tent, disappeared inside for several seconds, and returned carrying a leather satchel. Rummaging inside, he withdrew a clump of what looked like soft clay coated in a heaping globule of pine resin. He proceeded to divide it into four equal pieces.

"You might want to stand aside," he said to the other mercenaries. He then waited for them to move safely away before attaching the sticky substance to the four corners of the door. Once done, he looked over to Sereb-Meloch. "Not sure this is going to work. I just made it a few weeks ago, and haven't had a chance to test it."

"What will it do?" the high priest asked, more intrigued than ever.

The foreigner grinned and shrugged. "We'll see in a minute."

Reaching into his satchel again, Achelous withdrew a long piece of cord and cut it with his knife. After cutting four shorter strands from the string, he tied all four ends to the longer one and then plunged them into all four chunks of clay.

"I don't think I used too much sulfur, but just in case, everyone should stand back another twenty feet," he said while spooling the cord out and laying the end on a piece of flint he'd placed on the ground.

Zaidu and the others laughed. "Not your infernal mud again, Achelous. For the last time, I doubt any man—or door for that matter—has much to fear from your ridiculous goo."

Sereb-Meloch looked from the mercenary captain to the foreigner, then up at the clay now pressed tightly against the gate. "It will not damage the Gate too severely, will it? It is imperative that my prizes not be harmed."

Achelous gave him a strange look in return. "Doubtful. I placed the charges to blow outward, not in." He paused, pulling another piece of flint from a pouch on his belt. "Besides, I'm a bit curious to see these *prizes* of yours myself." With that, he thrust the flint down onto the cord, watched as it sparked to life, and stepped back. "You all might want to open your mouths and cover your ears."

The entire cadre of priests and warriors watched tentatively as the strange sparkly fire ate its way down the line. Only Achelous seemed to heed his own warning. After placing two fur cloaks on each side of the prince's head, effectively covering the boy's ears, he crouched down to one knee, opened his mouth wide, and wrapped his hands tightly over his own ears. Ten seconds later, the shimmering fire spread out in four different directions and began to burn against the clay.

BOOM-BOOM-BOOM-BOOM!

Four rapid explosions shook the very foundation of the mountain, creating a wall of smoke that reduced Sereb-Meloch's view to just a few feet. He was unable to see his men. Unable to see the bound prince. Unable to see the strange foreigner that seemed to have an uncanny ability to harness the power of the sun itself. Worst of all, he was unable to see the famed Gate of Shamash. The thought chilled him to the core.

"Foreigner! What have you done?" he shouted into the smoky haze. His lungs burned with every breath, but that was the least of the high priest's problems. He suddenly realized that he had not heard the words he'd just uttered from within his own skull. All that he could hear at the moment was the echo of some great bell ringing maddeningly in his ear.

Achelous is some sort of magus, he thought, waving away the smoke from his face. *Controlling both light and sound. But what does he want? What is he up to?*

His concern evaporated as quickly as the smoke, for as the haze blew away on the frigid winter wind, he saw before him a great gaping hole in the side of the mountain, where only moments before the gate had hung. He'd done it. The mage-warrior had succeeded in opening the doorway to the *Realm of Eternal Darkness.* And what darkness it was! As Sereb-Meloch gazed into the perfect blackness beneath the mountain walls, his ringing ears were forgotten. He could not help but wonder if they hadn't opened a portal to the Great Void itself—the primordial nothingness of reality before *She* had provided the essential ingredients of creation. Apparently, some of his men were pondering the very same thing, for three of them—two priests and a warrior— began carefully shambling toward the open maw.

"Stop!" he shouted. "Don't go any closer!"

But the same deafening ring must have affected them as it had him. None of them so much as turned to acknowledge his command. They simply inched closer to the darkened entrance. The mercenary, at least, had enough good sense to draw his sword as he approached. Not that it would do him any good against the two creatures lurking within the shadows. But Sereb-Meloch was not concerned with the safety of his men. He simply wanted to avoid any unnecessary confrontation with the goddess's children.

"I said *stop!*" he yelled again.

But it was too late. Without warning, a giant, spear-like arm shot out from the dark, skewering the nearest priest in the chest. The multi-jointed arm, coated in black, insect-like armor, lifted its victim off the ground and pulled him back into the void. Before the other two men could even scream, another arm swung out. Its serrated edges sliced through the mercenary's body from shoulder to groin, cutting him in half. An instant later, the sound of the second priest's terrified, pain-filled screams began to seep into Sereb-Meloch's consciousness, just as the creatures' arms struck out a third time, sending the pathetic man's broken body hurling through the air and over the edge of the eastern cliff.

At least my hearing is returning, Sereb-Meloch thought, as he began barking orders to his men. "Back away!" he shouted, absently stroking the archaic headdress. Though everyone was too distracted to notice, the strangely colored band around the headdress seemed to shimmer with an otherworldly blue-green light. "This is why we've brought the sacrifice. Move past the altar and watch as the gods emerge once more into the land of mortals!"

Whether his men's own hearing was returning or not, they did not heed his words. As one, a small group of the mercenaries roared in anger, lifted up their swords and rushed toward the exposed cavern. One by one, the men fell, struck down by two sets of twelve-foot-long, insectoid arms. Arms that in many ways reminded the high priest of some great mantis.

Before he could reflect any further on the creatures, another wave of men rushed into battle. This time, however, they'd learned from their brethren's mistakes. The moment that the carapace-covered arms lashed out, each man ducked, rolled and came up again, bringing their swords down against their attackers. Six heavy bronze blades swung down toward the offending arms, only to clatter uselessly against the armored hide.

Enraged, one of the creatures, still enshrouded in the cavern's blissful darkness, lunged forward, bringing both blade-like arms down on a single soldier and pinning him to the ground. The young man screamed in agony as the beast swept its arms out in opposite directions, ripping him apart.

The mage. Maybe he can bring this situation under control. Where is he? Before Sereb-Meloch could scan the chaos around him to find Achelous, his concentration was interrupted by a shout. Not the ear-splitting shriek of one of the mercenaries being torn to pieces, but rather a cry of outrage. The voice was familiar. Captain Zaidu.

Sereb-Meloch spun toward the distressed cry. Toward the sacrificial altar. His mouth jerked open the moment his mind registered what he was seeing. The foreigner had freed the prince from his bonds and was now in mortal combat with the mercenary captain and three other men.

2

Achelous's two curved blades flashed around in a swirling arc, clanging against the two weapons of the nearest mercenaries. Within five seconds, the two considerably lesser-skilled warriors lay dead in pools of their own blood. With the other mercenaries and priests occupied by the giant creatures still lashing out from the cavern's shadows, only Captain Zaidu maintained sense enough to deal with the real threat.

Bringing an ancient horn up to his lips, the captain gave a great blow and garnered his troops' attention. They turned to stare at the one-on-one battle.

The foreigner, keeping the prince behind him, whirled his swords, fending off Zaidu's sudden sword thrust.

"Traitor!" the captain spat. "I took you in. Fed you. Gave you purpose. And this is how you repay your commander?"

The foreigner's only response was to press the attack with a backhanded swing that nearly took Zaidu's head from his shoulders. Sereb-Meloch knew the move would be Achelous's mistake. With comprehension suddenly dawning on the captain's men, nearly twenty of them rushed to the aid of their commander. Five more held back, readying their bows and awaiting a clear shot. Before their comrades reached the fray, a swarm of arrows cut through the air and slammed full force into the foreigner. The bronze-tipped projectiles punctured the man's leathery skin with ease and burrowed deeply into his arms, chest and neck.

Plucking the darts out with simple jerks of his wrists, Achelous continued his offensive against the captain and his now, fully committed men.

Sereb-Meloch watched in amazement as Achelous's neck wound spurted out a geyser of blood that stained the pristine snow crimson. *A shame*, he thought. The man's intellect and courage would have made valuable assets. Instead, the man would bleed out in minutes. Sooner if the battle continued with the same ferocity.

But despite the extreme loss of blood, Achelous continued to fight with a nearly incomprehensible strength. Of the twenty mercenaries that had joined the fray, thirteen now lay dead or dying in the snow. Two more had suffered extensive, but not life-threatening injuries.

But that was nothing compared to the onslaught the foreigner continued to endure. The high priest's men hacked at the man, inflicting mortal wound after mortal wound. One swipe sliced cleanly through Achelous's throat, clear to the spine if Sereb-Meloch wasn't mistaken, yet still the man fought with the might of the hero-gods of old.

The thought unnerved Sereb-Meloch more than he wanted to admit. *Can it be possible?* Could it be that the gods, knowing what he intended to do, sent a champion to stop him from awakening the Mother? The very thought was preposterous, but how else could he explain it? A man who could control both light and sound, blasting a giant wound into the side of the mountain? A man who could endure blade and arrow alike without so much as slowing down? It was as if Marduk himself had descended from the heavens to thwart Sereb-Meloch.

Then why had the man—if that is what he truly was—helped to unleash *Her* children from their subterranean prison? Why had he used his magic to assist in the high priest's acquisition of the next vital piece of the plan?

A muffled grunt of pain drew Sereb-Meloch from his musings. He looked up to see the prince, secured once more by two more seedy-looking mercenaries. The foreigner was on his knees now, Zaidu's three-foot-long blade plunged deeply in the man's chest. Achelous's eyes widened, confusion and pain reflecting across his dark irises. A stream of blood spewed from his mouth as he heaved for breath.

They had done it. The mercenary captain had finally quelled the traitor's sedition. A wave of relief cascaded over the high priest. *Mortal after all. Not a god. Not a champion. Simply a lone fool who sought to undo everything I have worked for.* But that thought unnerved him as well. *After all, where there was one, there could be more...* How many other traitors were lurking within his ranks? He'd have to be more vigilant. For now, however, he would savor this new victory and watch the warrior-mage die.

As if sensing his master's unspoken thoughts, Zaidu stepped closer to his fallen foe, looking down into the man's pain-filled eyes. Without a word, the captain spat in the traitor's face, drew an ivory-handled dagger from his sash, and swept it across the man's throat. Whatever blood remaining in the man's body after the direct blow to his heart, poured freely from the smiling laceration. Satisfied Achelous was no more, Zaidu shoved the dead man to the ground with the palm of his hand and turned to face the high priest. With a glow of satisfaction about him, he gave a slight bow toward Sereb-Meloch, then turned his attention to the two creatures still preying on those stupid enough to get too close to the cavern's mouth.

The monsters roared from the shadows, yearning for the sacrifice that would draw them from the prison they'd called home for the better part of two millennia. Their chitinous claws lashed out from the shadows, desperately searching for their prey.

"The boy!" Sereb-Meloch shouted. "Get him to the altar now. There can be no more delays!"

Before his men could comply, a great shriek arose from inside the cave, followed immediately by the sounds of thrashing and even more howls of rage and desperation. From the sound of it, the creatures, Namtar and Tiamba, were locked in mortal combat. If Sereb-Meloch didn't act, they'd tear themselves apart.

Nervous, he turned toward the altar where the mercenaries secured Belshazzar's bonds once more. Satisfied all was ready, the high priest strode toward the open gates with arms outstretched. The headband glowed even brighter—practically blinding to those who looked directly at it—as he recited the arcane chant, exactly as he'd practiced it for the past eleven months.

"Acheno, le Baranaga! Acheno terana, Namtar eb Tiamba! Thret nasi, belagon Tiamat neastar trumpo! Eb learenok gonno, Belshazzar Erraga!"

Hear me, Great Ones! Hear my words, Namtar and Tiamba! Come forward, O' Children of Tiamat and feast. Behold the sacrifice, Prince Belshazzar of Babylon!

He smiled when the sounds from inside the cave ceased immediately. The months of studying the ancient language—words not uttered in over two millennia—had paid off. And now, he had gained the great creatures' attention and hopefully, their cooperation.

Sereb-Meloch stepped back, his eyes never leaving the dark cavern. Something shuffled from within. *They're coming!* The high priest stepped past the stone altar and gave a quick glance at the doomed prince. He would have the ultimate revenge against his old nemesis, the boy's grandfather, and claim his prizes with one swift blow. The joy of that revelation warmed his chilled insides, as he continued backing away from the cave.

A low growl echoed from the shadows, followed immediately by a giant, insect-like leg. Followed by another and another. Soon, a great mass of shiny black armor slunk from the cave's entrance, shrouded by the cloudy night's sky. The creature's form was truly monstrous. Six enormous spindly legs supporting the weight of a giant's torso. The torso was human in nature, but covered from claw to head in a hard-shell carapace. Two more limbs, attached at the creature's shoulders, folded twice—once upwards and then down, so that the blade-like structures assisted in balancing the creature while walking. Those gruesome features, however, were not what sent a wave of dread down the spines of all present. That honor was left to the creature's nineteen-foot-long tail, which curved to a point behind its back and dripped with lethal venom.

Girtablilu.

Scorpion Men.

That's what the legends had called them. Children of the enormous goddess Tiamat, from whose body all of creation had sprung. Feared and revered for ages untold, the Girtablilu were said to be as cunning as they were vicious. But they could also be of assistance to certain brave mortals not afraid to harness their power...as revealed by the tales of *Gilgamesh.* It was Sereb-Meloch's hope that he would be counted just as worthy as the immortality-seeking adventurer. All that remained to ensure their loyalty was the awaiting sacrifice.

A sacrifice of royal blood.

Amid gasps, everyone in the high priest's entourage moved back. Though many had been privy to the object of Sereb-Meloch's current expedition, few had actually believed the legends to be true. Now, as they watched the second scorpion-creature lumber from the cave, their skepticism disintegrated along with their false bravado.

The scorpion brothers scuttled toward the altar.

It was finally time. The sacrifice would be accepted, and their loyalty would be assured.

"Wow," came a voice from somewhere behind Sereb-Meloch. "As an old friend of mine would have taken great pleasure in saying, those are some big-ass bugs." Sereb-Meloch, Zaidu and nearly half the mercenary's men wheeled around at this new interruption, paralyzed with confusion and fear.

Standing, his sword resting casually on his broad shoulder, the foreigner Achelous looked back at them. The wound on his throat was completely gone; only the drying blood remained. He smiled mischievously. "Yeah, I know," he said. "What's it gonna take to kill this guy, right?"

3

"But how...?" Sereb-Meloch attempted to say.

Jack Sigler, the man once known by the callsign 'King' and now by the Greek name 'Achelous' said, "Step away from the boy. Now."

The time for the charade was over.

King had bided his time with this lot long enough. He'd wormed his way closer and closer into their inner circle, just to get close enough to the prince that he could affect a rescue when the time was right. He'd been at it for weeks, watching and waiting. Of course, he could have taken the kid any time he'd wanted, but he'd had a secondary goal as well. He wanted to know exactly what had gotten the priest all hot and bothered about this particular excavation. He'd heard rumors from the other men, of course, but he had to see it with his own eyes. Had to see the Scorpion Men for himself. He'd hoped he might learn what Sereb-Meloch's long game was, as well. After all, if he couldn't stop the priest right here and now, the intel would come in useful later on.

But things had started to get a bit hairy once he'd been forced to open the gate. He knew his time for recon was over and that a hasty retreat, with the Babylonian king's grandson in tow, was going to be the better part of valor.

Before anyone could process the supposed-dead man's resurrection, King dashed to the altar, drew his sword and sliced through the leather bonds for the second time in fifteen minutes. Taking the boy by the hand, he helped him off the stone slab. Before they could break for freedom, however, an enormous armored tail shot out from the right, nearly taking King's head off.

"Run!" he shouted, shoving Belshazzar away and pointing southeast. "Run as far away as you can. I'll catch up."

Without waiting to see whether the prince complied, he turned to face the two enormous arachnids, his sword gripped tightly in hand. He wished the weapon was an M4 with an attached grenade launcher. Even better, he longed for his old team. His friends. In his past, the world's future, King had faced monsters and madmen along with his team of Delta operators, using the best technology and weapons the United States government could buy.

But that was ages ago. Or ages *from now*, depending on how one looked at it. Still, during the two-hundred-plus years that King had been stranded in the past, wandering the world, he'd fought his share of gruesome, truck-sized monsters all on his own. He'd learned a thing or two about how to handle himself against such things.

One of the creatures swung a twelve-foot-long arm at him with blinding speed. Matching the speed, he rolled to the left, came up and struck at the appendage with his sword. The bronze blade did little more than rattle in his grip.

That's Lesson #2, he chided himself. *Find some iron weapons. When fighting giant monsters, swords made of bronze rarely ever do anything more than piss them off.*

He knew from his studies of history, before he'd come to the past, that he was sometime in the early iron age, but that didn't mean that lowly mercenaries had access to the best weapons. Bronze swords were still widely in use.

But he should have been paying more attention to Lesson #1. The first and key lesson he'd learned over all his time was: never let them hit you.

A second creature's tail whipped wildly through the air, its two-foot-long stinger impaling him in the gut, just inches from where Zaidu's sword had pierced him only minutes before. King's body was lifted off the ground. His feet dangled uselessly, nearly two feet from the snow-covered earth.

"Ah, shit."

He looked down at his abdomen, the stinger twitching rhythmically as it injected its poison into his system. He could feel the stuff shooting forcefully through his veins. His muscles constricted and convulsed as the organs of his body began to shut down.

No matter how many times he died, he never got used to it. Death hurt. Plain and simple. And this time was no different. The only thing he hoped for as he drifted off into oblivion was that the kid had managed to clear out and find safety. He would find the kid when he awoke again and got himself out of this mess.

Fortunately, he didn't have long to wait. Mere seconds after being flung from the scorpion's stinger, he felt his heart beating once more. He savored the sweet rush of air as it began filling his lungs. He tensed as his punctured flesh began knitting itself back together. When he opened his eyes, the Scorpion Men towered over him, their vaguely human faces scowling down at him.

4

The good news, from what King could determine from where he laid, was that Sereb-Meloch and his men were standing clear. They hadn't dared to approach the angry monsters, their sacrifice lost.

Slowly, he raised himself up onto his elbows and looked up at the monstrous brutes hulking over him. The sound of gasps from all around told him the crowd was once more surprised with his inexplicable return to life. Still, as long as the scorpion twins stood their ground, he was in little danger from Zaidu or his men. Which gave him a little time to think.

The creatures—King thought he'd heard Sereb-Meloch refer to them as *Namtar* and *Tiamba*—leaned closer, their nearly two-dozen eyes fixed atop their heads seeming to burn a hole straight through him. They appeared just as confused at his resurrection as the rest of the audience, which implied they were also sentient. Intelligent. Not monsters at all, but rather some sort of human-arachnid hybrid?

King had run across a few animal-human hybrids during his time in the past, the most well known being the mythical Minotaur in Crete a few decades ago. That one had been a mindless beast. Tortured through genetic experimentation by a madman claiming to be one of the gods of Olympus. A little pyrotechnics and a whole lot of good timing had taken care of it. But Namtar and Tiamba were different. They'd apparently inhabited that cave for over two thousand years, but despite their gruesome appearance, they didn't strike King as feral. Angry, yes. But not wild. They'd understood Sereb-Meloch's strange summoning. Had come forth when the priest had called them. *Perhaps I can reason with them?*

"Okay, let's take it easy for a second," he said.

Though their facial expressions were nearly non-existent, King could have sworn they flinched at his words. A better way of putting it was that they appeared startled. Had they understood him?

"I'm going to stand up now. I'm hoping we can have a conversation like three rational...people. Alright?"

Namtar and Tiamba growled a clear warning, glanced at each other and then took a single step back.

Keeping his eyes fixed on the two arachnids, King climbed to his feet, dusted himself off and gave a slight nod in their direction.

They launched into another attack, simultaneously slinging their tails in a clothesline that would have made any Red Rover line proud. But King had been ready for it. The instant they moved, he dove backwards into the snow, rolled and came to his feet with his sword in hand. Then he eyed the nearest creature carefully, scrutinizing every inch of its armored body. A determined focus spread across his bearded face, and he ran full force in his opponents' direction, dropped to the ground and slid between Tiamba's legs. Timing the move just right, he thrust his sword upward, slicing through a seam in the armor, between its right thigh and groin. His aim was true, and the blade cut deeply into the creature's flesh, eliciting a terrible shriek.

He yanked the sword free as his momentum propelled him past the howling beast. Once clear, he rolled to his side and scrambled up to his feet. The giant arachnid-men were already turning to face him; their shark-like teeth bared in angry grimaces. Black liquid gushed from between Tiamba's legs, covering the ground in tar-like blood.

"Kill him!" Sereb-Meloch screamed from a safe distance. King risked a glance in the priest's direction. A dozen archers were raising their bows.

They won't risk the priest's big prize, King thought, turning his attention once more to the greater threat, though he kept the creatures between him and Sereb-Meloch's men, just in case. *I just need a few more minutes...*

With a screeching howl, the injured and enraged Tiamba leapt, reaching ten feet into the air, and plummeting toward King with its deadly tail extended straight for his chest. There was no time to dive out of the away. King thrashed his blade in a leftward arc, deflecting the stinger. The creature's weight plowed King to the ground, but the stinger plunged harmlessly into the snow-covered rocky soil, just to his right.

"Son-of-a-bitch!" King shouted as he batted his sword against the creature's carapace. He was quickly losing his patience in this fight. The more time he wasted, the more likely the prince would be recaptured, and he just couldn't afford that.

Tiamba, having learned from their last encounter, pinned King to the ground with four of its spindly legs, being sure to keep the seams of its armor clear of his flashing sword. With a flick of its claw, it swatted the blade from King's hand, then leaned in to sniff curiously at King's face and neck.

King twisted his head away from the putrid stench emanating from the beast's mouth.

The creature raised its spear-like forearm and let it hover just inches above King's groin. Then, it cast him what could be described only as a malicious grin and let the serrated edge of the arm drop down into the upper portion of King's right thigh—near the exact same spot King's blade had pierced the creature.

King screamed. The pain was even more unbearable than when the other creature's stinger had pierced him through the gut. The serrated blade twisted, grinding inside his leg and cutting deeply into the bone. Tiamba's grin widened.

This is vengeance for the wound I inflicted. The thought erased all doubt about the monsters' sentience and chilled him to the bone. Fighting mindless monsters wasn't easy, but brains always trumped brawn. Brawn with brains...that was a different problem. A much more deadly problem. The realization turned his mouth and throat to cotton.

Or that could just be dehydration from rapid blood loss, he thought, as he writhed at the monster's prolonged torture.

A moment later, the pressure of the arm lightened, and the creature leaned even closer.

"KIIIIINNNNGGG," it hissed, being sure each expulsion of breath wafted directly into its prey's face.

King froze. His frantic struggling completely ceased, as his entire body went rigid. It had spoken. Had actually said his name. *Hadn't it*? But not just his name, his *modern* callsign.

"W-what did you just say?"

The creature's grin broadened, then it lifted itself from King and scuttled over to its companion. King's hand instantly shot down to his leg, trying to ease the pain of the wound, as he struggled to his feet.

"What did you just say?" he repeated, being sure to keep his eyes fixed on the two arachnids, while he scooped his discarded sword off the ground.

But the two terrifying creatures only stared at him vacantly, without reply.

"You really can understand me, can't you?" he asked in English. "How do you know my name?" Still, the scorpion men refused to answer.

Cautiously, he glanced around. Sereb-Meloch's men were all gawking at the strange confrontation. Even the high priest appeared transfixed. Though King hated to admit it—hated to give up an opportunity to discover more about the scorpion men's secrets—now was the best time to bug out and live to fight another day.

He would likely survive a prolonged encounter, but the prince might not. And the prince was what was important. The prince was everything.

He could already feel his injured thigh mending. The deep cuts to his bone had already healed over. He should be fine to run. At least, if the giant circus freaks allowed it. That was the big question. As they stood there, their shiny black carapaces gleaming from the moonlight bouncing up off snow, they merely looked at him. Curious. Their rage and malice sated.

But why?

King figured he best not look a gift-horse in the proverbial mouth. It was time to get out and find the kid. He'd worry about the why and the how some other time. The prince was his mission, and he never strayed from the mission. It was how things got done. He had to get Belshazzar back to Babylon and his grandfather—and not just because it was the right thing to do. After his little pirating adventure the previous year in China, he could use the reward money. Jian Zhou was not going to let his debt go any time soon, so the sooner he paid the pirate back, the sooner he wouldn't have to worry about the Chinese assassins following him across Asia.

Without warning, King turned to run. Neither Namtar nor Tiamba appeared interested in stopping him. He could hear no sounds of any pursuit as he bolted in the direction in which he'd told the prince to run. His sudden movements had, however, rallied the mercenaries to action. Shouts erupted from Zaidu, his harsh commands to his men to stop King echoing across the mountain top. Despite that, King kept running. Ignoring the cries for his surrender.

"Foreigner!" he heard Sereb-Meloch shout from fifty yards behind him. "Do not think for one moment there is any place on this Earth you can run to escape me. I will find a way to end your life forever."

Realizing he would soon be surrounded by Zaidu's men, King stopped, turned to face his enemy and drew his sword in preparation for what was to come. "You can try," he answered in Aramaic.

Without another word, he took off. Sprinting up the nearest incline, his blade was already in full swing before he reached the first squad of soldiers awaiting him on the apex. With three swift strokes, his opponents collapsed, their blood staining the pristine snow.

"After him!" cried Zaidu, as he huffed his way up the hill. "Do not let him escape!"

Twelve more men ran out from the tree line, their swords and spears leveled at King. The first man to reach him, a spear-wielder, feinted to the left, swiping the shaft of his weapon upward, in an attempt to impale King from the groin up. King dove away from the strike and directly into the path of three more men. Ducking a swinging blade, he rolled forward and came up again in a dead sprint. He didn't have time to play around with these guys. Every second he spent in combat was time wasted in finding the prince. His best plan of attack was simply to avoid fighting altogether, and that meant retreating as fast as his legs would carry him.

He could hear the soldiers pursuing him. Their fur-shod feet crunched in the six-inch-deep snow behind him, followed by cries of anger and dismay. King had had a few centuries to improve his conditioning. As a Delta operator and later as the leader of a special ops unit known as Chess Team, King had always been in top physical condition. But two hundred years of fighting his way through the ancient world had nearly perfected him physically. He was faster and could run longer than any human he'd ever encountered, as was evidenced by the fact that the sound of pursuit was growing fainter with every step he took.

He allowed himself a brief smile. He could see a rather gentle slope just over the horizon. Once he made it there, it would be a simple task to make his way down the mountainside and hopefully catch up with the prince.

For a moment, facing the scorpion men, King had wondered whether he was going to survive the encounter, but he now felt a measure of calm assurance return.

When his keen ears picked up the whistling sound coming from directly behind him, he knew his relief had come too soon. Before he could understand the sound's threat, his entire back side was bombarded with the blinding hot tips of nearly two dozen arrows. He plunged face down into the snow and died. Again.

5

"Hey daddy?"

"Yeah?" King asked, looking into the wide, brown eyes of his adopted daughter, Fiona.

"How many times can a guy die in one day?"

"What?" King felt a strange twist in his gut. They were sitting at a breakfast table. Somewhere familiar, but not. Was this Rome? The Coliseum filled the background view, but it looked restored.

"She's right, baby," said a soft voice. Sara, King's fiancée, slid up beside him, wrapping one arm around his chest and placing a plate on the table in front of him with her free hand. Her voice was like honey, but wrong. Different than he remembered. She was speaking Aramaic. "How many times *can* you die in one day?" She patted his chest. "Now, eat."

King looked down to see his own head resting atop the plate, staring back.

The dream snapped to black as King awoke, but he didn't open his eyes or even move. The dream was a hard one, but he'd had enough just like it that he no longer woke up violently. *They're right,* King thought, *how many times can a guy die in one day?* It wasn't the first time he'd wondered that, and he doubted it would be the last. Extreme situations seemed to seek him out. Or maybe it was the other way around? He did, however, hope it would be the last time he asked the question for a while.

Though his body had the uncanny ability to heal with almost instantaneous efficiency, making him practically immortal, it didn't change the fact that arrows—or swords or spears or falling off a cliff, for that matter—hurt like hell. And that was just the physical aspect of his condition. He shuddered to think of the psychological damage that was being done to him, every time he faced the cadaverous breath of the Grim Reaper.

First things first. Time to see how bad it is, he thought.

He hadn't opened his eyes yet. He wasn't eager to see whatever dire circumstances awaited him. He presumed that Sereb-Meloch's men had caught up to him, and probably dragged him back to the campsite. Maybe even laid him out on the sacrificial altar for good measure. *Time to face the music.*

Before taking a look around, he decided to let his other senses pick up on a few things first. A habit he had long since cultivated. The first thing he noticed was the intense light burning into his eyelids. The sun had risen. And from the position of the light, he guessed it was close to noon.

He could also make out the crackling of a campfire just off to his right. From the severe warmth on his face, he was pretty sure he was laying fairly close to it, because it was too chilly out for the sun to warm him that much. He could also discern that he was on his back, which meant that the arrows must have been removed. A shuffling sound a short distance away told him that someone was nearby, possibly keeping watch over him, waiting for signs of life to return, so the high priest could be notified. And finally, he caught the slightest whiff of something foul in the air. Excrement. From some sort of animal. A horse maybe. It didn't really surprise him. Zaidu's mercenaries had managed to get a few pack animals safely up to the summit of Mount Mashu. It stood to reason they'd be nearby, grazing on what little vegetation was not frozen by the eternal winter here.

He cracked one eye open and scanned the terrain. To his surprise, he didn't seem to be in any portion of the camp he recognized. For one thing, the dense stands of cedar trees appeared to be sparser here. Second, to his right, he could see Mashu's peak, high above him. Apparently, he was at the base of the mountain now.

How long have I been out?

There was no telling. There never seemed to be any rhyme or reason to the amount of time between his so-called resurrections. Stab him in the heart, he might wake up a day or two later. Drop a piano on his head, and he might be dancing a waltz in under five minutes. The amount of trauma or the way in which the injuries occurred had little, to nothing, to do with it. All he knew was that he had awakened in some of the strangest places anyone could possibly imagine—which at times, was even more unsettling than the whole 'dying' thing.

A soft gasp from behind him brought his thoughts back to his current predicament. Whoever had been lurking about had noticed he was now awake.

"*Katea non latrisy,*" spoke a soft, high-pitched voice in Akkadian. "*Etuo siri Ba'al Marduka niaban?*"

King was still picking up the language. Was far from mastering it, but he could get the gist. He turned his head in the direction of the speaker. As he'd suspected, it was the boy, Belshazzar.

"No, I'm not Lord Marduk," King answered as best he could. At least, he hoped that's what he said. "Just a soldier. Trying to get you home to your family."

The kid looked at him suspiciously, which was just fine with King. It gave him a chance to rifle through the loads of historical and mythological miscellanea Deep Blue, his former black ops handler and friend, had forced him to study while leading the Chess Team. If memory served, Marduk was an ancient Mesopotamian god. Depending on who you asked, he was either a benevolent protector or guardian, as the Babylonians told it, or he was a vile dictator and devourer of innocent children, as the Hebrews portrayed him. Either way, he was seen as a fierce warrior and champion of the other gods when they went to war with the mother of all gods... *What was her name? Tia-hut? Tia-nep? No, Tiamat.* He couldn't recall much more than that, other than that Marduk had apparently killed her and set himself up as king over the other gods.

So the question was why the boy wanted to know whether he was Marduk or not. Fortunately, he didn't have to wait long to discover the answer.

"If you are not Lord Marduk, how is it that you control the elements of fire, air and earth?" Mercifully, Belshazzar had reverted to the easier to understand Aramaic language. He moved into view, just as King edged himself up onto his elbows and attempted to sit up. His back burned, as though a thousand white-hot needles were jutting from his spine.

King stared at the boy for several moments before fully understanding the question. *The explosive I used to blow open the gate.* To the people of this time, it must have seemed like the work of the gods. Or magic.

"I don't control them. It's just science." He knew from history that the Babylonians were quite advanced in the sciences. It was a concept he was sure the boy would understand. "Chemistry. A little sulfur...er, brimstone is what you call it. A dab of zinc. Some pine sap, some clay and a few other odds and ends. Mix them together and you can get quite an—" King fumbled for the word. He wasn't sure there was one in Aramaic for it, so he switched to Greek and hoped the prince would understand. "—explosion."

Belshazzar nodded, but King could tell by the look on the boy's face that he was quite skeptical. "So how is it that Ba'aleti Ereshkigal could not take you despite all her attempts?" the prince continued, using the name of what King remembered to be the Babylonian goddess, or 'Lady' of the Underworld. A fancier name for the Grim Reaper. Death.

He took a good look at the kid and smiled. Perhaps 'kid' wasn't the best way of looking at him. In this world, he would be considered almost a man. Could be married off in only a year or two, if his family deemed it appropriate. He could even march off to war if necessary. No, he'd have to stop thinking of the prince as a child and more as a young man.

"It's a long story." King pushed himself off the ground and stood. His legs still felt like two sticks of rubber as he attempted to balance himself. "But trust me. I'm not Marduk. And before you ask, no, I'm not any other god either. Just a man that's tough to kill. If I was a god, that whole debacle up on the ridge would have gone a whole lot smoother."

Belshazzar still looked doubtful, but he didn't push the issue. He just pointed over to the campfire and smiled. "I prepared some food with which to break our fast. Some fish I caught in the stream over there. We still have several hours of sunlight left, but I say we should be moving well before the sun sets."

King glanced at the blazing fire. Its acrid smoke billowed up into the gray, noonday sky as high as he could see. Instantly, he spun around, scanning the horizon while simultaneously drawing his sword from its sheath. It was such a foolish move on the prince's part. The fire would surely draw Sereb-Meloch's attention. Even though the priest had insisted that Namtar and Tiamba couldn't venture out in the light, that didn't mean his own men couldn't be on the prowl even now. For all King knew, they were making their way toward the camp...

Wait a minute.

"The camp," he said, almost to himself. "Last I remember, I was running away from Sereb-Meloch's camp. I was shot by some arrows and fell. How'd I end up here?" He paused before adding, "And where exactly *is* here, anyway?"

Belshazzar gestured toward the food he prepared. "Do not worry about the heretic," he said, as he crouched by the fire and flaked off pieces of the fish onto a slab of wood he'd fashioned into a plate. He handed it to King and smiled. "Eat. Regain your strength. We have a long journey ahead of us." The prince waited until King had taken the food before explaining. "I must admit, I didn't exactly follow your instructions last night. I ran as far as the edge of the forest, but then I watched what happened to you. When you were shot, you were propelled forward, toward a slope. The snow carried you far down the mountain—a fall that would have certainly broken every bone in a normal person's body. I had despaired that you most certainly had not survived the descent, but to my surprise, you had. From that point, it was a relatively easy thing to fashion a gurney and pull you down the rest of the mountain, using the snow's help. I found a secluded spot to make camp and then waited for you to awaken—after I dressed your wounds."

"But Sereb-Meloch," King insisted. "Why aren't they..."

"Sereb-Meloch is much too focused on the last leg of his mad venture to worry about us," Belshazzar said. The way he spoke...the way he held himself...it was getting more and more difficult for King to see him as a child any longer. "He will send his assassins, I am sure. But for now, his main concerns are the Girtablilu demons—children of the dread Tiamat." The prince paused curiously and scrutinized King once more. "If you are not Marduk, how is it that Namtar and Tiamba ceased their assault on you?"

King swallowed hard at the memory. Had he heard Tiamba correctly? If so, how on Earth could they have known his callsign? How could a creature, locked away for centuries, more than three thousand years before he was ever born, know who he was? The questions unnerved him more than he liked to admit. Still, for the time being, he felt it best not to dwell too much on it. He was determined to get the answers, but for now, he'd let it go. He looked back at the prince and shrugged. "I have no idea what that was about. And honestly, I'm not going to worry about it." He wolfed down the fish, savoring the rich taste. It felt like eons since he'd last eaten anything. "Right now, my only concern is getting you home...to Nebuchadnezzar."

Belshazzar looked up from his breakfast to stare thoughtfully toward the horizon. Then he shook his head. "We cannot return home. Not yet."

"Why not? I went to a lot of trouble to get you out of there. The king has offered a very promising reward for you, and though I'm not ordinarily a mercenary, I could use the money." He paused before adding, "Besides, it's my nature, but I won't feel right until I know you're safe."

The boy turned to look at him. "This reward... How did you hear about it?"

It was a strange question. King wasn't entirely sure of the relevance, but he saw no harm in answering.

"A caravan a few weeks ago. Merchants traveling from Babylon. They told me you'd been taken while on a hunting trip with your cousins." King paused. He'd also heard that Belshazzar's cousins, along with two bodyguards and three attendants, had been killed during the kidnapping. This kid had been through a lot for someone so young. "The caravan chief told me about the reward, and the rest is history."

The prince smiled at this. "And this merchant did not specify the terms of the reward?"

"He didn't really need to. A king's grandson is kidnapped. The king offers a reward for his safe return. Simple."

This turned the boy's smile into a deep throated laugh. "Perhaps where you come from. Or perhaps, if said prince was anyone other than Acolyte Prime to Ba'al Marduk."

"Um, I'm not exactly following you."

"The reward. It is not for my safe return, but for my assassination."

6

The old eunuch bolted up from his bed. Sweat glistened down his brow as he struggled to catch his breath. The dream had been so intense. So vivid. It wasn't the first time Yahweh Rohi had induced such a vision to guide him. In fact, such dreams had led him to the very place he now found himself—third in command of the great Babylonian empire.

It wasn't even the first time he'd seen the 'stranger' in his dreams. A man from another world. Another time. A fierce and skilled warrior with a heart of rare nobility and honor.

However, it was, he had to admit, the first time he'd felt such dread after one of these visions. Something was happening. Something the world had not seen since the rescue of Mosheh or even Noach's great flood. And, as he'd predicted nearly six months before, it was all tied to the good prince and the blasphemer Sereb-Meloch.

The king's greatest fears were coming to pass.

The old man climbed from his bed and moved hastily to the basin to wash his face. His mind's eye was still ablaze with the nightmarish images. A fallen temple of iniquity had arisen from the sands. Bodies of man and animal alike had been strewn here and there, their blood building into a great river of crimson. Fires had canvassed the horizon for as far as the eye could see, and a tempest of sand and lightning cut through the air like a saber, as the sky turned to the blood red of death.

Prince Belshazzar had stood in the center of it all, as the eye of a fierce storm that would rip the world apart.

The only uncertainty in the entire dream was the part the stranger would play. The old man had seen the stranger battling warrior and demon alike, with a ferocity he'd not seen in his long life. But then the sands had seemed to swallow him whole, and the strange man had disappeared into obscurity.

"What is it you would have me do, Lord?" the old man whispered softly to the empty room.

But he knew the answer already. No need for his God to provide any more instructions. He'd trusted in Yahweh Yireh for the better part of his life and he'd never been disappointed. He'd not start doubting now that he was approaching the winter of his years.

He knew what he had to do. Of course, he'd have to do it without the king's knowledge. Nebuchadnezzar would never sanction such a venture. After all, he'd already sent out his assassins to prevent this catastrophe from happening. He'd certainly balk at the idea of his most valued advisor interfering with his royal decree.

But the man known by his own people as Daniel had a decree issued from a king far higher than the royalty of Babylon. He would not fail in obeying the command of Yahweh, even if it meant his own death for treason against the king. After all, the destruction of the very world was at hand, and only he knew how to prevent it.

7

Sereb-Meloch raged throughout the camp. With the foreigner's interference, he'd lost both his prized sacrifice and the dead of night, which had allowed the Girtablilu to travel openly. Granted, the priest had been instructed exactly how to overcome their nocturnal preference. But the setback angered him nonetheless.

"Ba'al, our scouts have been unable to locate the foreigner or the prince," Jereziah cowered as he spoke the words, his attention frozen on the hulking monstrosities that stood on either side of the high priest. "Zaidu and I have sent out more men. With dawn approaching, it should be easier to..."

Sereb-Meloch's headdress began to glow ominously, and before the portly priest could finish his sentence, Tiamba's saber-like arm slashed down, impaling the man with a single swipe of the claw.

"I do not tolerate incompetence, Jereziah," Sereb-Meloch said to the man, who now lay dead on the snow-covered ground. "You should know that by now." He glanced up at his scorpion men and gave a brief smile. "You may have him."

He headed for his tent and didn't look back as the creatures tore at the fallen man, the sound of ripping flesh echoing wet and sickly in the pre-dawn gloom. The sounds matched his mood, which was growing darker by the moment.

This setback required prayer. The goddess would be most displeased with the news, and he shuddered to contemplate the reprimand he'd face when he informed her of this man Achelous, and the failure to sacrifice her enemy.

Captain Zaidu stood at attention at his tent's doors. The man's face had turned a ghastly green, as he'd watched the Girtablilu feast on the fat man, several yards away. *Good*, Sereb-Meloch thought, *let that be a lesson to him as well.*

"Well?" Sereb-Meloch demanded of the mercenary captain.

"I have sent scouts ahead to all the nearby cities and villages," Zaidu said.

Sereb-Meloch thought he heard the slightest trace of a tremor in the man's voice, now. "The way I see it, they will need horses. Supplies. Babylon is some distance away, and they will not get very far without those things. Which means they will be making their way to the nearest settlements, west of here. The village of Susa is the most likely place. Once they do, my men can track them and send back word on their whereabouts." He paused. "We will find them. I have no doubt about that."

The high priest looked the soldier up and down with disdain. "For your sake, Captain, you best hope so." He briskly waved the man aside. "I will be in my tent, in prayer. See to it that no one disturbs me."

The mercenary saluted as Sereb-Meloch stepped past him and into his tent. He removed the headdress and other vestments, then stripped down to his undergarments. He lit the sticks of incense at the altar near his bedding, as well as an oil lamp that hung from the wooden beam of the tent, and dropped to his knees.

Calming himself, he began to meditate. He focused on the flame of the lamp, the sweet aroma wafting from the bars of incense. He withdrew into himself and allowed the world around him to dissolve. Soon, he began to hear his own voice resonating in a deep strange tongue he'd never learned. A chant to summon the spirit of his queen. His goddess.

I AM HERE.

He wasn't sure how long he'd been meditating before the strange voice arose in his mind. It could have been seconds. It could have been days. Time had no meaning when in her presence.

"My Queen," Sereb-Meloch said out loud. If Zaidu's voice had harbored a slight tremor, his own was outright quaking. Whether from fear or joy, he wasn't entirely sure. "Do you know what happened?"

For a long while, there was nothing but silence. After an eternity, the voice—which oddly resembled his own—spoke again inside his mind.

I HAVE SEEN THROUGH THE EYES OF MY CHILDREN.

Whether she was angry or not, the high priest could not be certain. Her voice was always so stark. Dispassionate.

"I am truly sorry, my Queen. I will make this right. I will destroy the foreigner and recapture the..."

KKKIIIIINNNNNGGG.

King? No, he was about to say 'the prince.' The king was too well protected. It was why the boy had been chosen instead. But before he could say this, the goddess spoke again.

KING INTRIGUES ME. INTRIGUES MY CHILDREN. MY HATEFUL, REBELLIOUS CHILDREN.

"Not the king, my Goddess," Sereb-Meloch said. "The prince, you surely mean. We will reclaim him soon. I give you my solemn vow."

THE PRINCE...THE CHILD OF MARDUK...WILL BE MINE SOON ENOUGH, the voice inside his head said. *BUT KING IS NOW MY DEMANDED SACRIFICE. KING WILL BE THE ONE TO OPEN MY TOMB AND RELEASE ME FROM MY SLUMBER. TO UNLEASH MY DESTRUCTION UPON YOUR WORLD.*

"But...but my Queen, how is it possible? My men would never be able to take Nebuchadnezzar. We would never..."

NOT HIM. THE MAN YOU CALL ACHELOUS.

The foreigner? A king? But that made no sense. Why would a king be working as a hired mercenary?

YOU WILL CAPTURE HIM. YOU WILL KILL HIM.

"He has proven rather difficult to kill."

I WILL INSTRUCT YOU ON WHAT YOU MUST DO. MY CHILDREN WILL THEN GIVE HIM THE KEY, AS A FINAL ACT OF REBELLION AGAINST ME. LET THEM. IT WILL BRING KING TO ME.

The high priest didn't understand. If the man was dead, how could he open the tomb? How could he do anything at all? Still, he would trust in his goddess. He would do what she said and would reap rewards greater than any mortal had ever imagined possible.

"And the prince? What would you have me do with him?"

Another long pause. For the briefest of moments, Sereb-Meloch feared she had departed from his tabernacle. A wave of relief washed over him when she finally spoke again.

BRING HIM TO ME. THE CHILD OF MY ENEMY MARDUK WILL BRING ME NEW LIFE.

Sereb-Meloch knelt in his tent the rest of day and deep into the following night, as his goddess shared many things about the days ahead.

8

The Zagros Foothills, East of the Town of Susa

"So if I'm not taking you back to Babylon, where exactly *are* we heading?" King asked as they trudged along the snowy plain west of the mountains. He was beginning to like this mess less and less with every new piece of information. He was also still having a hard time wrapping his brain around the fact that Belshazzar's own grandfather, King Nebuchadnezzar, had issued a contract for his death. Even after the prince had explained it to him—twice—he was still completely bewildered by it all.

"To the ruined city of Eridu," the prince said. "The city was founded millennia ago by the great Nimrod, said to be the earthly incarnation of Ba'al Marduk himself. Eridu is where the tomb of Tiamat is said to rest. We must get to it before Sereb-Meloch and the Girtablilu."

King struggled to grasp the wisdom of going to the exact place their adversary wanted the boy to go. The one place that had marked the prince for death by his own royal family. It turned out that Belshazzar was not only heir apparent to the throne of Babylon, he was also an acolyte for the god Marduk. The chief acolyte at that. As the two had packed up camp and prepared for the long journey west, Belshazzar had explained that it wasn't only his royal blood that had caused Sereb-Meloch to target him as a sacrifice for the Girtablilu.

"Sereb-Meloch is a high priest of a blasphemous cult of Tiamat worshippers," Belshazzar had explained. "It is his belief that she is not actually dead at all, but merely in slumber, like a great bear that hibernates in winter. He believes it is his divine calling to awaken her. If he does this, she will feed upon the life-giving elements her body released upon her death—elements that were used to construct the world all around us. In short, she will unmake everything in existence, if returned to life."

The rest, King had managed to piece together from his studies in mythology, additional nuggets revealed by the prince and even a few things he'd picked up while infiltrating Zaidu's band of mercenaries. Before the universe existed, there had been the gods. And like all pantheons of antiquity, they were all a bunch of a soap-opera debutants and backstabbing SOBs. Tiamat, the mother of them all, waged war on her children—the lesser gods—after they had assassinated her husband. In turn, they sent out a champion, Marduk, who eventually defeated her.

Marduk had cast her body out into the void, and the universe had been born from her decomposing flesh. From what Belshazzar had told King, the myth was only partially true; the full story, known to only a handful of Marduk's high priests, had been passed down orally through the generations. From what King gathered, the goddess had been buried in a primordial stone. Marduk had erected a great prison, disguised as a temple, to secure her for all eternity. While she slumbered, however, it is believed that parts of her essence—King assumed it was something like atoms, from the description he'd been given—seeped from her rocky sarcophagus, thus bringing about the earth and the rest of creation.

The only thing capable of unsealing the tomb, Belshazzar had told him, was a key...a key that would be revealed by the blood of the warrior-god Marduk, or as King's luck would have it, by his 'Acolyte Prime.' In other words, Prince Belshazzar. The sacrifice to the scorpion men was meant to appease them and garner their favor, while providing the necessary ingredient to open the sepulcher of Tiamat. Nebuchadnezzar, of course, knew the danger his grandson's blood represented, and the Babylonian king had been willing to do whatever it took to keep the deranged priest from opening the tomb—even if that included murdering his own grandson.

Apparently, Belshazzar believed Sereb-Meloch had traced this tomb disguised as a temple to a place called Eridu. It was the last place on earth they needed to be, and it was the first place the crazy kid actually wanted to go. *Damn. We're bypassing the frying pan and jumping right into the fire.*

Apparently, the prince could detect the mental battle raging in King's mind.

"I know it sounds mad." Belshazzar took a swig from a water bladder and then handed it to King. "But I cannot return home now, no matter what. Not until the threat of Tiamat's tomb is ended once and for all." He looked up at King, his eyes wide with worry and fear. "I cannot do this alone, Achelous. I need your help."

That one bewildered and frightened look helped remind King that despite how grown up or how brave the prince might seem, he was still just a normal twelve-year old boy. A child. An innocent who could not possibly survive this on his own. He would need help.

The people of this time and this world referred to King as 'Achelous.' He'd not taken the name of his own volition. Ninety-three years before, he had overthrown an evil despot in a small settlement, near the outskirts of Athens. The people had been overjoyed at their newfound freedom. Like many before and since, they had felt his deeds were those of a god. When he'd insisted he was not, they tried to make him their king. After his insistent refusal, they'd done the only other thing they could. They'd bestowed on him a name of great honor...the name that in Greek meant 'He who drives out grief.'

King had accepted the name with humility and grace. Since that time, he'd done everything he could to uphold the gift those poor villagers had conferred upon him. Now, looking down at Belshazzar's haggard and fearful face, he knew to continue to honor that gift, he really had no choice. He would see this boy through the coming ordeal, no matter what. He'd become he boy's protector. His soldier. His guardian.

"All right, I'll help," he said after an uncomfortably long pause. "But first, we're going to need some horses."

9

The City of Nippur, Two Weeks Later

King felt uneasy. He'd been so ever since entering Nippur, a thriving religious center a few days journey west of the Tigris River. When they'd entered the gates earlier that afternoon, the city, famous for its grand temple to the wind god Enlil, had been teeming with pilgrims, traveling merchants, soldiers and the assorted swarm of humanity so common across the fetid infrastructure of such places in the region. The throng, pushing and shoving their way through the narrow, stone-cobbled streets, had made it impossible for King to tell whether he and Belshazzar had entered unnoticed. A handful of unsavory types were always lurking about, but it was nearly impossible to tell whether they'd taken any interest in the newcomers.

King had, of course, insisted that Belshazzar cover his face with a tagelmust—a long strip of cloth wound around the face and head to protect the wearer from harsh desert hazards, such as sandstorms, intense heat and the sun's blazing glare. Wrapped around the prince's face, King thought it should at least protect the boy's identity for a time.

Now, set up for the night inside the city's only public house that still had space available, he was beginning to worry. He'd ordered the prince to remain in their room until he could secure food and drink for them both. The plan was to stay for the night, recuperate from their arduous journey and then hit the road before dawn the next morning. But sitting in the cedar wood chair, waiting on the tavern-keeper's daughter to prepare their meal, he scanned the crowd huddled together in drunken debauchery within the dingy tavern.

Just as in most public houses of the region, this one was dotted here and there with some of the most weathered and homely prostitutes King had ever seen. Their portly arms wrapped casually around the necks of every cutthroat mercenary and vagabond that ventured into the place, desperately trying to lure the road-weary travelers into a night of decadent bliss. The ones actively engaging the harlots were no bother to King. It was the handful of men who managed to ward off the prostitutes' charms that concerned him the most. From one corner of the room to the next, King spotted at least six sets of dark eyes locked squarely on him, clayware mugs of ale practically untouched.

King's eyes darted to each man, instantly assessing the impending threat level. To his left, at the table nearest the exit, sat a swarthy man of lithe frame, clothed in rough leathers. His sash held no less than six small daggers and one curved scimitar. A quiver of arrows adorned his back, though King couldn't locate the bow that was undoubtedly nearby.

Further across the room, leaning back in his chair, so his massive head rested against the stone wall, sat a giant of a man. King estimated this one at nearly seven feet tall and weighing around three-hundred and fifty pounds—the weight was comprised mostly of muscle. King couldn't detect a trace of fat anywhere on the huge man's frame. Strange markings—possibly tattoos—covered much of the face not hidden by his bushy mane of a beard. His hands, too, were almost matted in hair, and King got the distinct impression that this was someone from the frigid climes of the north. Perhaps Russia. He could see no weapons anywhere near the man, but with his size and brutal demeanor, King couldn't rule the man out as a potential threat.

At the table directly across from him sat three men locked in quiet conversation. Though outwardly they showed no signs of malicious intent, King had been tracking them the longest. He'd glimpsed one of them near the city gates, when he and Belshazzar had first entered the city. The other two had been loitering near the bazaar they had passed, coming to the inn. Since King didn't believe in coincidences, he was pretty sure their presence here was ominous, to say the least. The simple fact that they hadn't taken their eyes off him since the moment he'd come out of his rented room, confirmed it. They were up to something, though there was little King could do about it until they made their move.

Finally, the most unnerving watcher of all was the ancient man hunched in his chair, to King's right. Shrouded in the same desert rags so common among the nomadic shepherds of the region, the man would have seemed innocuous enough if his eyes hadn't constantly darted to the same men King had been eyeing in quick, furtive glances. The old man's gnarled fingers rubbed nervously at his cup, while he mumbled unintelligibly to himself in a language King could not quite place. Since King had spotted him, the man had not once looked in his direction. Instead, he kept a constant vigil on the others, as if anticipating the danger that lay ahead.

There was no doubt about it. Despite King's best efforts, he and the boy had drawn entirely too much attention to themselves. Between Nebuchadnezzar's assassins and Sereb-Meloch's warrior-priests, there were simply too many unknown variables to keep the prince safe while in a heavily populated city.

After more than thirty uncomfortable minutes, the barmaid came out to King's table brandishing a healthy plate of roast mutton, steamed dates wrapped in grape leaves and some strange concoction that resembled mashed potatoes that had been mashed just one too many times. Paying the doe-eyed barmaid, he gathered up the plate and a flagon of ale, and carried it to his room. As he strode toward the door, he became more and more convinced of the need for a change of plans. If they remained in their room through the night, the prince would be dead by dawn. *Time to get out of here.* They'd eat, pack the leftovers for later, then slip out of the city before anyone noticed. They'd then find a safe place outside the city to camp. Somewhere remote, with sufficient cover.

His new plan went to hell the moment he opened the door to the room. Belshazzar was nowhere to be seen.

10

A mountain-sized lump swelled in King's throat as he darted into the room in search of his charge. Tossing the food onto a nearby table, he began shoving the room's sparse furniture aside, hoping the prince had hidden under the bed or the cupboard. The room had only one entrance and no windows. There was nowhere for the kid to hide. A tense ten second search revealed nothing of Belshazzar's whereabouts.

"Shit." King spun around and retreated back out into the common area. Of the initial six stalkers, only the three congregated at the table together remained. The Russian, the archer, and the old man were nowhere in sight. "Shit. Shit. Shit," he mumbled to himself in English, gripping the hilt of his sword as he scanned the tavern.

"I'm gonna kill him," he growled, as he began making his way to the door. Before he'd made it five feet, the three loiterers stood from their table, and made their way in his direction.

"Where do you think you are going?" one of them, the largest and most heavily armored of the group, asked.

He drew his sword from his belt, and his two buddies followed suit.

"I don't have time for this," King said. Before the other could respond, King stepped to the larger man's left and extended his left leg around the other's while throwing a swift upper cut across his jaw. The man wheeled backwards, tripped over King's extended leg and slammed into a nearby table, crashing to the wooden floor with a thud. King spun around with a roundhouse kick, knocking a second man to the ground before leveling his sword at the third's throat. "I suggest you let me pass."

The third man, his eyes wide, nodded before backing away and opening a path to the door. Taking his cue, King dashed out into the dusty street and glanced around. With the sun having set hours ago, the streets were dark. Only dotted here and there with the occasional torch lamp, attached by a sconce to the side of a building. A gentle, but arid breeze brushed past King's cheeks, drowning out any subtle sounds of movement he might have otherwise heard. The city had cleared of almost all traffic. Only the occasional intoxicated wanderer scuttled along the manure-littered streets.

King's heart thumped harder against his chest. How could he have lost the boy? If Belshazzar had left of his own free will, what had he been thinking? Why would he have left the safety of the room? What possible motive would there have been in that?

King's memory drifted back to the first moments of entering the city and fast forwarded to the time he'd discovered the prince missing. He hoped to find something that might shine a little light on the boy's sudden disappearance, maybe insight to where he might have wandered.

The kid had been captivated by the town. Awestruck by its architecture and tightly winding streets. Having grown up in Babylon's palace, he'd never been allowed to walk among the capital city's people. He'd never been permitted to experience life in the big city. From the moment they'd stepped through the gates, the prince's eyes had expanded with wonder at all the sights and sounds. The stench of the desperate masses. The emotional tsunami of the mob-minded crowd crashing through the city gates with them.

So of all the kid's wonder, what had garnered the most of his attention?

As King allowed his eyes to wander around the city once more, they caught sight of a structure jutting above the canyon of squat, sandstone buildings surrounding him. A strange parapet, like a twisted stone finger pointing accusingly toward the sky. King knew the parapet would lead down to the base of a massive ziggurat temple dedicated to the Mesopotamian god of wind and earth, Enlil.

Of all the structures the boy had seen, the ziggurat had been the one he'd insisted they visit. He'd explained that as Acolyte Prime of Marduk, it was his holy duty to pay homage to the lesser gods whenever approaching one of their temples. But King had refused. The city was far too dangerous for a sightseeing expedition, even one of religious observance. King had ushered Belshazzar away, toward the center of town, in a ramshod search for a place to stay the night.

The temple would be the one place the kid might have slipped away to see. Unfortunately, it looked like the prince's escape had been unobserved by King alone. If the missing stalkers were any indication, they'd ducked out the moment King had left the room. Once again, coincidences and King never saw eye to eye. Belshazzar was being hunted. Perhaps already caught.

King sprinted southeast toward the temple. A five minute run through the narrow, winding streets brought him directly to the base of the enormous stone pyramid. The massive gates leading to the temple were left unguarded, and King wasn't certain whether that was a stroke of luck or a terribly bad omen. With the influx of travelers and pilgrims making their way to the city for the annual festivities honoring the wind god, he'd expected a certain amount of security to be in place, discouraging thieves and cutthroats from the buffet of easy pickings. At the very least, he'd thought they'd be there to keep the peace among the ever increasing intoxicated throng.

Just outside the gates, several caravans, their camels and pack animals bedded for the night, huddled around a cluster of campfires all around the ziggurat's protective walls. He could hear men praying and singing praises to appease their god. Forty-five hundred years before, when Nippur was constructed, Enlil had been the chief deity among all the Mesopotamians. Not only was he the god of earth and wind, he was also said to have created humans. As Nippur passed down from empire to empire, the city— and subsequently, its temple—had seen various states of disrepair and renaissance. Eventually, as the Babylonians had come into power, Enlil was replaced as the chief god by Marduk.

Still, even today, Enlil was seen as an important figure, especially to the nomadic shepherds and tribesmen, who could easily be doomed by the sudden rage of an unexpected sandstorm. To survive, the people would do anything required to appease the god of the wind, including this annual pilgrimage to his temple to pay homage and sacrifice.

King quickly began scanning the crowds, searching for any signs that his charge had huddled among the throngs to pay his own form of respect. But as King made his way around the temple's perimeter, searching by the dancing illumination of the campfires, none of the travelers came remotely close to resembling the young prince of Babylon.

If he'd come here at all, he was either hiding from King's watchful gaze or he'd entered the temple proper. As King looked up at the marvel of masonry engineering, he scratched his head, wondering where the architects would have constructed an entrance. He supposed the most reasonable place would be at the very top, at the apex of the structure. If he remembered his prior studies correctly, the uppermost structure of the ziggurats were typically reserved for shrines to the gods to whom they were dedicated. If Belshazzar had indeed come to pay his respects to the wind god, he most certainly would have headed there.

Looking up at the daunting climb before him, King couldn't help wonder about the stark differences between the religious zeal of history versus the cushy comforts of modern religion. King knew people sometimes had a hard enough time convincing their loved ones to attend services every Sunday...and modern churches had easy access wheelchair ramps and elevators. He could hardly imagine the state of affairs if the world-weary church goers of the 21st century had to climb the two-and-a-half-foot high steps of a ziggurat each week. Then again, King supposed that was probably why the pilgrims only came annually to pay their respect.

Taking a resigned breath, he passed through the gate and began climbing the steep incline, which jutted nearly one hundred feet into the air. Hand over foot, he slowly crawled his way toward the apex, praying the boy would be there, while simultaneously hoping, for Belshazzar's sake, he wouldn't be there, to avoid any temptation to throttle the boy for worrying him like this.

The climb, however, hardly winded him, and by the time he reached the temple's entrance he had already recuperated most of his strength. Having the metabolic regenerative powers of a demigod did, King had to confess, have certain advantages.

He ducked through the open entrance and rushed into an open chamber, lit by twelve torches.

The prince stood in the center of the room, surrounded by six armed killers wielding swords, knives and clubs.

11

At that moment, King knew where the gate security team had gone. Four of the six rough-looking men wore the bright, colorful raiment of the temple guards. The other two were the Russian, wielding a rather large wooden club, and the thinner man in leather King had seen at the tavern. Thin Man's skeletal hands clutched two lethal looking daggers. As he spun around to see King, his right hand instantly released its blade and hurled it directly at King's chest.

King had been ready for it. He couldn't afford to die right now. Every second he was down would make it that much easier for the bad guys to kill the kid. Darting to his right, the knife whizzed harmlessly past his head to embed itself into the mortar of the wall behind him.

"I'm going to let that slide," he said, his hands raised in a placating gesture. "But the next man to move on me, or my friend, is going to have his head separated from his shoulders."

"Achelous, do not antagonize them," Belshazzar pled. His brow furrowed with deep concern. "The large one is called Balyah, and he is one of my grandfather's most favored warriors." Balyah snarled at King, as the boy continued. "You may or may not be a god, but in Balyah's native land, his godhood is unquestioned and Death is his domain."

King looked the man up and down, then shrugged. "Death is every man's domain. Some of us just arrive sooner than others."

Balyah growled something unintelligible and his men leapt into action. The Thin Man instantly hurled his remaining daggers in King's direction, just as the four temple guards turned their swords on him. Drawing his own blade from its scabbard, King parried each of the thrown knives with three deft flicks of the wrist. He then met the maelstrom of the guards' flashing swords with a flurry of well-time deflections, followed immediately by a kick to one assailant's groin. The man doubled over, dropped his sword and fell to the floor in agony.

When King looked up from the writhing guard, he saw Belshazzar grasped firmly in Thin Man's serpentine arms. The man cast King a wild, toothless grin before placing one of his knives to the prince's throat.

Seeing this, King doubled his efforts, using fighting techniques that wouldn't be developed for thousands of years. Two swings and a single stab of his sword brought the remaining three temple guards to the floor. Blood oozed into pools beneath their still bodies. Leaping over them, he lunged toward Thin Man only to be blindsided in mid-air by the telephone pole of a club swung by Balyah. The blow brought him crashing to the floor in a heap, with at least three broken ribs and a shattered rotator cuff. He wheezed for breath, struggling to remain conscious. Fighting to stay alive. If he lost it now, the boy was as good as dead.

"Not bad," he said between a coughing fit of blood and bile. *Add internal bleeding to the diagnoses.*

With his one good arm, King pushed himself off the ground to face the bear of a man with the club. Balyah's furs seemed to bristle, as if there was still life in them, as they draped over his massive frame.

"You are strong. Good," Balyah said in broken Aramaic. His accent was thick. Strange. King couldn't place it from all his travels, but he was certain of his original assessment that the barbarian was from a region near Russia. "Will be more pleasurable to crush you this way."

King glanced from Balyah to Thin Man, the latter's blade drawing dangerously close to the prince's throat, as he watched the exchange with gleeful malice. King hoped that the boy would be safe as long as the knife-wielding assassin was kept entertained. Of course, that meant King would have to make this fight with a would-be god of death interesting. Considering the inhuman strength the proto-Russian displayed with that club swing, King didn't think it would be a simple task. The guards had been easy enough to kill. Thin Man wouldn't be much of a challenge, once it came down to it. But Balyah was another thing entirely.

The big man hefted the club just before lunging with a powerful swing. King ducked left, spun and brought his sword up to sweep toward Balyah's trunk-like legs. But the big man's size belied his speed. Before the blade could connect, Balyah leapt into the air to sail harmlessly over the blade. As gravity pulled him down, his cudgel flew directly at King's head. King managed to swat the blow away with a sweep of his sword, but the impact shattered the weapon in two, leaving King defenseless. He leapt back from another swing, unable to counter it.

The one living guard, now apparently recovered from the groin kick, hobbled to his feet, picked up his fallen sword, and ran from the chamber. King wasn't sure whether the man would stay clear of the fracas now or if he'd run to gather reinforcements. Either way, King was running out of time. He needed to wrap this up quickly, and he wasn't sure how to do that without a weapon.

Balyah laughed. It was a deep, rumbling guffaw that nearly shook the foundation of the temple and sent spittle dripping through his thick black beard.

King glanced around for anything he might use as a weapon. Bare-fisted, he wasn't sure he could take Balyah. The man's strength was astounding. His speed and agility were equally inhuman. His physical similarities to King's friend Alexander, the historical Hercules, was so striking, King wondered whether there might be something to the whole 'god of death' thing after all.

"Why you not give up?" Balyah asked after his laughter subsided. "You no match for my might. Let Balyah take little pup of prince, and you might live to see the dawn."

Still searching the chamber for a weapon, King's eyes locked on the perfect choice. "Because," he said, inching back toward the wall behind him, "I'm not big on backing down from fights with cocky trolls." At that, King swept his arm up, grabbed a torch from a sconce on the wall and leapt forward. The flame flared from excess oxygen, as it swept through the air at Balyah. The big man's eyes widened as the torch's burning light rushed at his face.

Unable to counter the attack, the torch struck the big man directly across his face, sending him reeling back. The torch's tip, wrapped in linen and soaked in pitch, gave the new weapon the heft needed to make a decent mace. Throw in the implied threat of incineration and King now had himself a very effective psychological weapon. After all, what bearded man was not afraid of having his face catch on fire from drawing too close to a flame? King knew, of course, that there was nowhere near enough fuel on the torch's head to do anything like that. But then, the torch was only phase one of his plan.

Now on the offensive, King put every ounce of energy he had into blow after blow with his improvised mace. Balyah, unable to recover, stumbled back even further, nearly slipping on the pool of blood left from the temple guards. The Russian recovered his balance at the last minute and remained standing, just as King dove forward and slammed his foot down hard against the side of the man's knee. A loud crack echoed through the chamber, followed by a wailing, unearthly howl.

Balyah crashed to the stone floor. His club forgotten, both of his meaty hands clutched at the shattered joint as he writhed on the floor. King pointed to Thin Man as a warning not to move, as he strode casually to the other side of the room, picked up a wooden pail and dumped its oozing contents all over the giant's battered body.

"You know what I just dumped all over you?"

Balyah, growling with pain, nodded once.

"It's pitch," King said, as if his opponent hadn't answered. "And you know what I'll do to you if you move?"

The Russian nodded once more.

King looked over at Thin Man and raised the torch over Balyah. "Let the boy go."

Thin Man hissed at the threat. Come to think of it, King hadn't heard him speak since their encounter had begun, and he wondered whether the man might be mute.

"What makes you think I care about that oaf?" he finally said with a toothless sneer, obliterating King's speculation about the man's ability to speak. Still, his voice was a grinding abomination of a sound, like a garbage disposal filled to the brim with clockwork gears and ball-bearings. "Who is to say I am not a god in my own right?" A long, fork-like tongue flickered past Thin Man's lips as he grinned. King had seen something similar before—on a trip to Seattle during a bar brawl he'd gotten into with a handful of tattooed, body-altering aficionados. He wasn't impressed then. Nothing had changed about his attitude now.

King tensed, visualizing a sequence of events he believed could free the boy, but not without considerable risk.

"Enough!" a strong, baritone voice shouted from the temple's doorway. King turned to see a weathered old man, stooped low at the shoulders, striding boldly into the chamber. Though he'd been unable to see much more than the man's eyes earlier, King knew that this was the same elderly man who'd been skulking about the tavern.

The old man's eyes blazed with fury. As the newcomer glared at Thin Man, then down at the fallen Balyah, he stood up straight. The bend in his back was now a straight line of determination.

"Gramel and Balyah, you know who I am, I presume," the old man said. His voice was rich, deep and commanding.

The two men nodded sheepishly. Their eyes glanced down, avoiding the elder's gaze, as if he might consume their very souls with nothing more than a wink.

"Then know this," the newcomer continued. "The prince and his guardian are under my protection now. The king's bounty might be great, but you know for whom I speak...and his wrath is not worth ten thousand such bounties."

Like scolded children, the two nodded silently again.

"Gramel, help your brother to his feet and leave this place now." The old man seemed to grow in stature to loom over the pair. "I will not ask again."

With trembling hands, Thin Man—Gramel—hustled over to the pitch-covered giant and helped haul him to his feet. Though Balyah's injured knee must have been shattered by King's blow, the giant managed to bear much of his own weight while his brother worked his way under the big man's arm for support. Without a word, the two limped from the chamber, leaving the wooden club and several discarded knives in their wake.

A smile cracked the dour expression on the old man's face, as the two scrambled through the door and onto the steep steps of the ziggurat. Then, after satisfying himself they would not return, the old man wheeled around to face the bewildered King and Belshazzar.

The old man clapped his hands together. "Oh my," he said, suddenly laughing. "I cannot believe that worked. I thought for certain the big one might have just as easily ripped my arms from their sockets than relent to my authority." He clapped his hands together again with obvious amusement. "Oh, glory be to Yahweh-Yireh...the Lord Who Provides, eh King?"

King started at the casual use of his callsign.

"What did you just call me?"

"I called you 'King,'" the old man said, a look of confusion plastering his face. "That's what you are called where you are from, is it not? Or do you prefer..." He lifted his eyes to the sky as if in thought, then rolled his tongue around his lips, as if tasting his next words before uttering them. "J-Jack, is it?"

King's heart slammed against his chest. For the second time in recent weeks, his real identity—an identity he would not possess again for another twenty-five hundred years or so—had come up out of thin air. First it was the scorpion creature. Now, this old man.

"How...how do you know that? No one should know those names."

"But, Achelous, this man knows everything," Belshazzar said. "There is nothing under the stars of heaven or the earth beneath that he is not privy to."

"A wizard? Is that what you're saying?" King didn't take his eyes off the old man.

The elderly man laughed at this and shook his head. "Oh no. Nothing quite so crass," he said. His smile was genuine. Warm. Not an ounce of deceit or contempt behind it. "I'm just a humble servant of the great Yahweh, Creator of all that is."

King looked away from the old man to search for Balyah's abandoned club. "Right."

"He's telling the truth, Achelous," Belshazzar said, sidling up to King. "He is the wisest man in all of Babylon. A seer. An interpreter of dreams and a mighty prophet of God."

"Which god? Marduk?"

The prince shook his head. "There are some gods even greater than my Lord Marduk. This man serves a god, Yahweh, who seems greater than all others."

Sudden recognition hit King like a truck full of anvils in a Wile E. Coyote cartoon. This time, however, the recognition hadn't come from the hours of study he'd spent as a Delta operator or with Chess Team, but rather from a place much more mundane. Sunday School as a child.

"Wait a minute... What's your name?"

Belshazzar looked at him puzzled, as if everyone in the world should know the answer to such a simple question.

"This is the chief magistrate of all of Babylon. Third in command of the entire empire," the boy said quietly. "Daniy-yel. His name is Daniy-yel."

12

"This is *the* Daniel?" King couldn't believe what he was hearing. Years of unwanted childhood Sunday School lessons flooded through his mind. "As in Daniel and the Lion's Den? The Writing on the Wall? All that stuff?"

Daniel laughed. "Oh yes. But my banishment into the den was years ago. Seems a lifetime ago, now." He stopped for a second and cocked his head to one side, as if puzzled about something. "But this 'writing' you speak of... I do not recollect anything like that. Perhaps it is something that is still to come in *my* future." He paused again, then let out a single bark of a laugh and clapped his hands again. "Ha! I have a future. That is good to know, certainly. Sometimes, I am not certain I have much time left...especially after disobeying his Highness's orders regarding the boy's assassination. His Highness will be most displeased about that, I am sure."

If Daniel was concerned, King couldn't read it in the man's face. It practically beamed with its own luminosity.

Despite coming face-to-face with a bona fide historical figure, King's thoughts remained on a single question. "You still haven't explained to me how you know my name. My *real* name."

"That is quite simple," Daniel said. His face grew suddenly sober as he ducked under the temple entrance to look out. "I have been having dreams of your coming for some time. Dreams of the prince's danger. Of the possible—but not inevitable—destruction of the world. And, of course, of the warrior from a different world that would serve as Belshazzar's protector. Yahweh-Yireh always provides. And he has provided me with many visions of a man who was both a king and not a king."

"So, you've had visions of me? Is that how the Girtablilu knew my name as well? Did your God give *them* dreams as well?"

Daniel's face whipped around from the doorway to look at King, his eyes wide. "The Girtablilu? You've encountered them?"

"Yes, Ba'al Daniy-yel," Belshazzar said. "Nearly a fortnight ago now. The Blasphemer has released them from Shamash's Gate. He intended to use me as a sacrifice for them. It was there that Achelous rescued me and agreed to accompany me to the forbidden tomb, before Sereb-Meloch's forces can release the great Tiamat."

"And when I fought them, one of them called me King. How do you suppose that is?"

"How indeed," the old man said, almost mumbling to himself in deep thought. His eyes developed a far-away look. His mind apparently contemplating the news's implications. "But perhaps that is something for us to discover another time." He glanced outside the entrance once more, then waved to King and the prince. "For now, I say we best be on our way. The temple guard who escaped your blade will likely return with reinforcements. And I would not put it past Balyah and his brother to regain their nerve and return to finish what they started."

Although he still had questions, King agreed with the prophet's reasoning. Scooping up Balyah's club, he moved over to the door and peered out. Not seeing anything of significance, he turned to Belshazzar and jabbed a single finger into the prince's chest. "If you ever...*ever*...take off on me again like that again, I'll hand you over to the first set of slave traders we come across. You got that?"

The prince nodded his agreement, and King turned once more to the narrow entrance. "You see anything?" he asked Daniel.

"It is quiet," the old man answered. "The pilgrims have all but disappeared." He looked over at King, his face strained. "Which does not bode well for us, I am afraid."

"You think the big guy and his scrawny brother are out there?"

"I think someone is. As to who, I am uncertain."

King gave one last glance out and shrugged. "Well, can't you just call up a vision or something?"

Daniel shook his head. "It does not work that way. A prophet of Yahweh is not a soothsayer or diviner. The Lord provides when he deems it best to provide."

King sighed. "This is exactly why I don't have much use for gods in general. They're never in much hurry to lend a hand when it's really needed."

"Do not be too quick to judge, warrior," Daniel said. "He brought me to you when you needed me most, did he not? And you to Belshazzar."

"I had it under control."

The old man laughed quietly at this, then stepped out into the night without another word.

"Do you trust him?" King asked Belshazzar, before allowing the boy to follow.

The prince nodded without hesitation. "With my life."

King let the prince pass and took a deep breath. "I suppose that'll have to do for now," he mumbled to himself. "But I'd much rather have a bazooka than a crazy old man by my side."

He stepped out into the night and began making his way down the steep decline to the temple's foundation. The moment his foot touched solid ground, he felt it shake.

13

The earth trembled beneath his feet, throwing him off balance. In the distance, toward town, bone-chilling screams broke out from the suddenly awakening masses. A trumpet blared, followed immediately by a great unearthly roar.

"It's the Girtablilu!" shouted Daniel. "They've found us!"

How on earth has everyone and their mother tracked us so easily? King wondered as he hefted the massive bludgeon onto his shoulder. *It's like we have a neon sign on our backs.*

King leaned forward to peer past the temple gates, but could see nothing of the scorpion men yet. "Is there a back door?"

"The priest's gate," Belshazzar said. "It is underground. It allows the priests to enter the temple unseen."

"Perfect. Daniel, take the prince and get him out of here. Forget the horses. Sereb-Meloch will have men watching the stables. Just leave the city as best you can. Head southwest, and I'll catch up as soon as I can."

"Wait. What are you going to do?" asked Belshazzar.

"I'm going to make some noise," King grinned. "Hopefully draw them away from your escape."

"But why?" the prince asked. "The priest entrance is perfect for hiding our escape from prying eyes. There is no need to take a stand now."

King looked from Belshazzar to the old man, who nodded his understanding.

"Come lad," Daniel said, placing a gnarled hand on the prince's shoulder. "Achelous is correct. Though the tunnels will certainly hinder their pursuit, it would not be enough. Your journey to Eridu must remain a secret. From Nippur, you might just as easily be heading home. But if Sereb-Meloch, or worse, your grandfather, surmises your true plans, no resources would be spared from stopping you. Your Guardian is going to lead them away in a different direction, I suspect."

More shouts of terror echoed through the city streets. They were closer this time.

King nodded at Daniel's deduction and turned to the prince. "I don't plan to fight for long. It might be difficult to kill me, but I don't believe I'm immortal either. No need for unnecessary risks. I just want to lead them in a different direction."

Belshazzar stood silent for several seconds before nodding. "All right," he finally said. "I will go with Daniy-yel. But you must survive this, Guardian. Without you, all hope of stopping Sereb-Meloch from releasing Tiamat's destruction is lost."

Daniel looked at King. "Just west of the town of Fara, there is a system of caverns near the entrance to a series of strange-looking rock formations. You cannot miss them. Look for us there when you've made your escape."

An inhuman roar exploded from just outside the temple gates. The horrendous cacophony was followed by another rumble in the earth. "Go. Now!' King shouted, grasping the club tight in both hands. "We're out of time."

Without argument, the old man and the boy dashed off in the other direction, disappearing in the darkness behind the ziggurat. King hefted the massive club and ran toward the temple's main gate. Just as he reached the fifteen-meter-tall entrance, an explosion of brick and masonry blew him backwards. He landed on his back, five feet away.

Shaking his head from the indirect blow, King looked up to see a storm of dust and powdered mortar swirling all around him. As a soft breeze blew the cloud away, he slowly began to make out the form of two giant creatures lumbering toward him through the wide hole in the stone wall. The creatures' long, serpentine tails bent backwards behind their human-shaped heads as they hissed.

Tiamba and Namtar drew closer, their hideously deformed faces resembling masks of fury and hate. Between them, walking casually, as if the temple grounds were his to call home, was Sereb-Meloch. A cruel smile twisted across his face.

"They are most displeased with you," the High Priest of Tiamat whispered. "You helped their prized sacrifice escape his fate. Their wrath remains unsated. Unfocused. They demand blood...as much as they can consume until the prince fills their bellies." He watched as King clambered to his feet and dusted himself off. "I suppose your mongrel blood will have to do for now."

King's eyes quickly scanned his surroundings, peering past the two brutes and their master. Though the gate had been widened by the Girtablilus' fierce attack, the way was now completely bottlenecked by the mercenary Zaidu and his men. The only way out would be the route Daniel and Belshazzar had taken, which would negate the entire purpose of King having remained behind.

No matter which way he played it, he could see only one possible outcome—his death. But King was determined to take as many of them with him as he could. Without uttering a word, he ran straight for Sereb-Meloch, bringing the club back as he did. The high priest shrieked in surprise, tucking himself into a protective ball. He needn't have bothered. Before reaching the cringing man, one black-armored scimitar of an arm lashed out, batting King away, as if he was a child's toy. For the second time in as many minutes, he was hurled backwards. The club slipped away from his grip, as he crashed to the ground.

Before he could recover, Tiamba pounced. Leaping nearly ten feet, the arachnid creature extended its arm directly toward King's torso as it dropped from the sky. Rolling out of the way, King scrambled to his feet, rolled toward the creature's left flank and jumped onto its back. He clambered up Tiamba's torso and wrapped both arms around its massive neck, putting the beast in a monstrous sleeper hold.

Tiamba roared as it twisted and bucked against its unwanted rider, but King's grip held firm. Putting every ounce of strength he had into it, King tightened the hold, attempting to choke the monster. With the segmented armor running up the Girtablilu's neck, he wasn't sure he was doing anything other than annoying it. But at least from this position, he knew Tiamba wouldn't risk using its stinger, for fear of striking itself. Sereb-Meloch's men and Namtar, wouldn't risk injuring the other creature either. And every second they wasted with King was another second Daniel and the prince had to slip away unnoticed. So for the moment, King figured he held the advantage.

But the moment didn't last long.

Without warning, Tiamba dashed forward, running full speed toward the immense temple wall ahead. The creature twisted, raised itself up onto its hind legs, and crashed backwards into the stone masonry. King was wedged between the beast and the wall for a split second, before being flung through the air. He landed on the sun-crusted earth with a resounding crack, and he felt something pop within him. He couldn't be sure what it was, but from the intense shooting pain from somewhere inside his gut, he figured it was nothing good. Heaving for breath, he tried to stand before the monster twins could resume the offensive, but his legs wouldn't budge. He could move nothing below the waist.

His spine had been broken.

14

The two Girtablilu stalked over to him, their tails swaying back and forth like cobras mesmerized by a flute. From between the protection of his two enslaved beasts, Sereb-Meloch strode up to stand near King's feet. Recovered from his earlier fright, the high priest glared down at his enemy. Hatred and venom radiated from his dark eyes, as he laughed at his fallen foe.

"You have failed, foreigner. Your diversion here has achieved nothing. I anticipated the prince's escape route and set guards at the other end of the tunnel. By now, the brat should be in their hands."

No mention of Daniel, King thought. A ray of hope attempted to flutter to the surface of his foul mood. *Maybe the priest doesn't know about the old man.*

"So the question," continued the lanky priest, "is what do we do with you? You are not a god. I would certainly know if you were. Though you have proven impossible to kill." Sereb-Meloch stepped forward, placing his booted foot on King's useless legs. Putting his full weight on the left tibia, he applied pressure until the air around them echoed with a loud crack. With the severed spine, King mercifully couldn't feel the leg break. "And yet, you *can* be injured, can you not? You can be damaged. And I would hazard to guess that you could be damaged far beyond your body's ability to repair itself."

"Possibly," King said between grinding teeth. "But know this: if you're wrong, if you fail to kill me... I'll put you through the same suffering times ten before this is over."

The high priest leaned down to glare at King. "Oh, I do not think that will happen. I know precisely how to deal with you." He glanced up at Namtar. "Bring him. I cannot defile this sacrifice to the Mother by killing him on soil dedicated to an inferior god."

Namtar growled its disapproval, but Sereb-Meloch held his ground. "Do not disobey me, beast. Your goddess would not approve of your rebellion now."

King couldn't help wonder what the high priest meant by 'rebellion *now*' as he was lifted into the air and placed across the creature's wide shoulders. Before he could dedicate any mental energy to the puzzle, however, he succumbed to his extensive injuries and slipped into unconsciousness.

King wasn't sure how much time had passed when he awakened to full consciousness. He'd slipped into and out of consciousness many times since being carried from Enlil's temple. His spine had stubbornly refused to repair itself during his slumber. This, of course, told him that A) he had not died since his last encounter with the Girtablilu and B) they couldn't have been traveling much longer than a day or two. His regenerative abilities would have mended even the most severe of bone fractures if it had been any longer than that—or if he had died. For some reason, a complete death sped up the recuperation.

He turned his attention to the more immediate concern of his current predicament. His head hung toward the ground, his face pressed against the chitin-like armor of the scorpion man's back. From this vantage point, he could see the creature's insectoid legs scuttling along a deep bank of sand.

"Achelous!" The voice sounded like Belshazzar, but King couldn't see the prince from his position. "You're awake finally."

"Bel? Is that you?"

A pause. "Yes. They were waiting for us when we emerged from the priests' way. They hurt Daniel. Left him there. I am not sure if he is alive or dead."

King twisted his torso, trying to get a better view. But the Girtablilu tightened its grip across his back, keeping him in place.

"Where are we? How long have I been unconscious?"

"Two days march," the boy said. "I do not know where we are, but I think we are drawing close to Fara."

There was a shout from behind King, and the creature suddenly halted its march.

"The procession is stopping," Belshazzar said. His voice was nearer now. King turned in its direction to see a small wheeled cart, complete with a wooden cage, which was being pulled by a donkey. The boy sat cross-legged inside the cage. "I cannot see very far ahead. I do not know why we have stopped."

"I can guess," King mumbled to himself more than anyone else.

Confirming his suspicions, he heard the strained, rasping voice of Sereb-Meloch from the front of the processional. "Namtar, bring him to me."

King looked over at the prince, as the creature began making its way toward its master. "Don't worry about me. Just do whatever you have to do to survive this. Understand?" His eyes narrowed at the boy. "Just survive. I'll come for you soon."

King was carried another thirty yards before being lifted from Namtar's shoulders and gently placed face up on a flat stone. For the first time, he was able to get a relatively good look at his environment. Unfortunately, there wasn't much to see. Desert stretched for miles in every direction. To the east, close to a mile away, a series of rock formations rose from the earth like giant teeth. From this distance, he could just make out a narrow pass between the rocks.

That must be where Daniel had planned our rendezvous, King thought.

"Now foreigner," Sereb-Meloch said, as he waded through the sand and approached the rock slab on which King rested. "We have wasted enough time with you. I have taken you far enough away from Enlil's city to avoid his wrath. It has given me ample time to study some of the tablets from my library, and I do, indeed, know how to dispatch you now. Permanently."

King looked up at the man, but refused to speak. Anything he said now would seem as if he was pleading for his life. He refused to give the bastard the satisfaction. Instead, he concentrated on his legs, willing them to move. Praying his spine would repair itself in time. He just hoped the pompous blowhard would keep talking long enough for his regeneration to kick in.

"...a most interesting study," the high priest was saying, when King returned his attention to the man's diatribe. "My goddess herself shared some of the secrets with me. The sacred texts. It seems there have been a few of your kind lurking in our midst through the centuries. Creatures of the darkest magic, unable to be killed by conventional means..."

King felt the big toe of his right foot shift within his boot. His heart rate surged with sudden hope. *Just a little more...*

"...two centuries ago, a rather impressive mage discovered an ordinary means of disposing of your kind. A cruel, painful means, but effective nonetheless. Any idea what it was, Achelous?"

King could no longer hold his tongue. "Sex with your mother?"

It was a childish retort, but the enraged flare from the priest's eyes made the immaturity well worth the gamble. Drawing the sword from his belt, Sereb-Meloch thrust the blade deeply into King's abdomen and twisted with all his strength.

"Watch that tongue, foreigner, or I might just remove it and keep it as a memento of your death." Sereb-Meloch favored King with a cruel smile. "I have always wondered what the afterlife would be like, if one is unable to speak. I might just put it to the test with you."

The searing pain in King's gut made it impossible to concentrate on the threat. Blood rushed from the open wound as the priest withdrew the sword. King's hands clasped futilely at the wound in an attempt to stem the flow of fluid. The slight tremor of his left foot went unnoticed by all but him.

"I truly wish I could savor your death for longer," Sereb-Meloch goaded. "But my goddess calls me, and I will humbly admit that you are just too dangerous to leave alive. So I will tell you the secret that dark mage discovered, all those centuries ago. He learned that if an immortal creature is beheaded, then set ablaze—their ashes scattered by the four winds—there is no returning from that. There is only death."

Captain Zaidu sidled up to the priest, just as the man had finished his explanation, casting a disgusted glance in King's direction. The mercenary brandished a large axe that gleamed in the noonday sun. Following close on their captain's heels, four more men advanced, carrying bundles of twigs and debris they'd obviously been collecting along the way, to be used for the fire.

"Do you expect me to beg for my life?" King asked, glancing past the motley crew in search of young Belshazzar. The boy's eyes clouded. Tears began to stream down his cheeks, as Zaidu's men busied themselves setting up the kindling. King turned back to the priest. "This is your last chance, Meloch. If you do this, I swear to the one and only God that matters... I will make you suffer more than you ever imagined possible."

The high priest's mouth opened as if he was about to say something, then closed. He looked over at Zaidu. "Do it."

The mercenary stepped forward, raised the axe above his head and lined up the best trajectory. Suddenly, King's legs pulled up toward his stomach and he sprang. The heel of his boot caught Zaidu just under the chin, sending the mercenary sprawling. Taking advantage of the surprise attack, King rolled from the slab, scooped up the fallen axe, and flew to his feet...only to collapse again in a heap. His spine, the broken leg and the most recent evisceration were all simply too much for his body to handle. Complete healing would take time, which was something he didn't have to spare.

Zaidu's men jerked King off the ground and dragged him to the slab once more. He was simply too weak to resist. The mercenaries tossed him unceremoniously onto the hard surface. One of the men spat an Akkadian curse before walking away.

"Namtar, Tiamba, hold him down," Sereb-Meloch said. "It is time we rid ourselves of this unholy vermin."

The two Girtablilu lumbered over to King. Three legs from each monster lifted and settled down on each of King's limbs and his torso, pinning him down to the slab. The scorpion men each looked down at their prey, but the animosity they'd shown before was completely gone. In its place, King could detect nothing but sadness.

As Zaidu dusted himself off and retrieved the heavy axe, Tiamba leaned its massive head closer and sniffed at King's battered body. It was the second time the creature had done that. The first had been when he'd first encountered them on Mount Mashu. Namtar followed his brother's example, leaned in and joined in the strange sniffing ritual.

"My lord, what exactly are those beasts doing?" Zaidu asked Sereb-Meloch, as he approached the slab.

"I imagine they are saying farewell to their last great hope," the priest replied.

Though dangerously close to delirium from pain, King puzzled over that last remark. 'Rebellion now'? 'Last hope'? Were these creatures being used against their will?

As if answering his unspoken question, Tiamba reared back. With a sound reminiscent of a lobster shell cracking, the creature's chest plates began to separate. Everyone's eyes grew locked on the scorpion man, as the plates spread farther apart. Two tiny, human-like arms extended from the crack. Underdeveloped, three fingered hands held something within their grip. Slowly, Tiamba lowered itself down and placed the object on King's heaving chest. King tried to see what the object was, but he couldn't even manage to lift his head. He clutched the object tightly and tried to bring it up to his face, but he simply didn't have the strength. The only thing he knew for certain was that it was flat, round and made of a shining, reflective metal of some sort.

"What is that? What are you giving him?" Sereb-Meloch demanded. Worry dripped with each word from the priest's mouth. But the moment the priest moved closer to investigate, Namtar whirled on him with a sharp hiss.

"It will make no difference, beasts!" the priest said. "He will be dead soon enough. And your trinket will be incinerated with him."

Satisfied that no one would make a move for the object again, Namtar returned to his vigil over King's pain-wracked form. Once the two creatures' full attention was again completely on him, they both leaned closer.

"KKKIIIIIINNNNNGGGG!" they hissed in unison.

King's heart skipped at the sound. There it was again. No mistake this time. They'd called him by his callsign. *But how is that possible? What is going on?*

"Enough of this!" Sereb-Meloch's shout pulled him back to reality. "Zaidu, end this now."

Without another word, the mercenary captain stepped forward. He eyed the Girtablilu warily, but stood his ground nonetheless. When they failed to prevent him from approaching, he raised the axe over his head and brought it down in one clean sweep. King's hands still gripped the strange Giltablilu object, as his head rolled to the left, off the stone slab and onto the dry, barren earth.

15

The darkness was everywhere. It was everything. It encompassed the entire world with its thick ebony silk. There was nothing else. No air or gravity or even earth. The darkness was complete. It was eternity, and King found that he really didn't mind.

There was a certain kind of peace to it. The weight of all he'd been through had suddenly been ripped from existence, and there was a cold comfort to that. A finality that lifted the burden of the world off Atlas's shoulders.

Since being tricked by Alexander those many years before, King had died and been revived countless times. Death had become such a part of his life, he'd long since learned to deal with the mental scars it left behind each time.

But this was different. Never before had he been aware of his death after the fact. Never had his conscious mind worked while his body lay dormant. It had always seemed like sleep. He'd drift off, only to awaken sometime later, refreshed and ready for another fight. This death, however, was like none he'd experienced before. His awareness of the darkness was proof enough of that.

He tried to remember what had led him to this point, but nothing was there. Tried to remember his past, but only brief flashes illuminated his mind's eye. A girlfriend—no, a fiancée. He had a fiancée now. A daughter too. He knew he had a daughter. Knew he loved her more than anything in the world, but for some reason he couldn't remember her name. And his team. He belonged to some sort of team, but their names and their purpose eluded him.

Oddly, only two names remained clear in the darkness of his death. *Alexander*. Or was it Hercules? After an eternity of pondering that question, King decided it didn't matter. The only name that mattered now would have turned his blood to boiling magma, if he still had blood to boil.

The second name was *Ridley*. An enemy. More than an enemy, in fact. King felt in his gut that no longer existed that there were few men, if any, that he could truly say he hated. But the man called Ridley would have qualified. King was certain of it. But that wasn't why the man's name sprang to mind here in the netherworld...in the darkness of his own death. There was something very important about that name. Something pertinent to his current predicament. Something essential that he needed to remember.

A sudden flash of white hot bronze blazed across his field of vision. Fire burned at his neck. His throat. His brain screamed silently, as a thick, metal axe head slammed down on his ethereal neck, splitting him in two.

What had the tall, lanky man said he would do? Cut off his head...and then what?

Ridley's name came to mind again. That infernal, cursed name. He'd been like King. Only different. Twisted. Corrupt. Not just where it truly mattered...not just in the soul...but corrupted bodily as well. Yes, like

King, Ridley had been able to die and return. Often. As a matter of fact, King had killed him on more than one occasion. Gruesomely, if memory served. And still, the man continued to come back.

Perhaps King was mistaken. Perhaps the darkness was playing tricks on him. Messing with his mind. His memories. Maybe King only fantasized about the horrible ways in which he'd caused the man named Ridley to die. It had been so long ago, after all. An eternity. Or was it only two hundred years or so? Time meant nothing in the darkness.

There must be a reason the man's name kept creeping into King's consciousness. A reason such a vile memory was attempting to reach the surface of the deep pool in his mind. After all, he'd much rather be thinking of his daughter. Or the woman he loved. What a travesty that he could not recall their names, but Ridley was forever etched into his soul.

Why is that? he wondered.

His subconscious screamed the answer at him. No matter how brutally ravaged the man called Ridley had been in the past, he'd always pulled through. Something like decapitation was nothing to him, so why would it be a problem for King, who'd been blessed with the pure elixir that Ridley had struggled to halfway emulate in life?

Another image. A blinding, searing flare of intense light blazed against his lidless disembodied eyes. The light invaded the wondrous darkness, burning. Biting and licking. The heat sweltered and stung. He felt it tearing into the flesh he knew he no longer possessed. Felt his limbs blister and melt, pouring off of a slab of stone like grease from a George Foreman grill.

The tall, lanky man had said something else. What was it? He would sever King's head from his body, and then to ensure he'd never return, he would...

What would he do?

Suddenly, King's eyes snapped open. They stared straight ahead into his own immolated torso. Flames danced all around him, burning his flesh into smoldering ruin. He tried to scream, but he had no more voice. How could he? His head had been removed from the rest of his body. No air could stimulate his vocal cords to elicit any sound. And still, the monstrous flames lapped at him with unforgiving teeth.

His boiling eyes watched in horror, as the skin of his chest blistered and cracked. Charred black. The epidermis split, revealing tender red meat, as his body broiled in the open flame. All the while, King could feel every cell—every atom—in his body screaming for mercy from the unforgiving fire.

Then, before he knew what was happening, something yanked him from the flames. First his head. Then, the rest of his body was heaved off the stone slab and onto the dirt. Smoke obscured his vision, making it impossible to see what was happening or who had extricated him from the funeral pyre.

Suddenly, all was darkness again, and King wondered whether he'd succumbed once more to the blackness of death. But there were other sensations in this darkness that quickly negated that theory. There was a course roughness of the darkness against his face. A harsh pain as the darkness lifted and came down upon him again. Someone was using a horse blanket to smother the flames. The agony was beginning to subside, though his face and body still smoldered in char and ash.

After an inestimable amount of time, the blanket was pulled aside and a lean, hunched figure knelt down beside him. The figure was mumbling something, but King couldn't make out what was being said. Then, mercifully, King closed his eyes, and all was darkness once more.

16

"Don't try to move," said a voice from somewhere in the distance. King heard it clearly, but it sounded far away and irrelevant to the excruciating agony that tore through his body. Disobeying the unbidden command, he tried to sit up, only to be rewarded with a horrid crunching sound and a sliver of torment unlike anything he'd ever experienced before.

He screamed, then felt a moist cloth come down across his forehead. "I warned you not to move," the voice said. "Your body is still pretty charred. You have lost most of the fingers on your left hand and the entire lower arm on the right. If you try sitting up like that again, something else is bound to fall off. So lay still."

King tried to open his eyes, but the lids were so stiff, like a wall of granite had suddenly materialized to replace them.

"Wh-who ah you?" he croaked. His throat was parched. Not enough moisture to form the words correctly.

His savior chuckled. "Already forgotten about me, eh? The Lion's Den? That writing on a wall, you mentioned?"

Daniel. It was Daniel. He'd survived the attack by Sereb-Meloch's men. Silently, King thanked whatever God the man worshipped for the not-so-small miracle.

"H-how b-bad?" he asked, giving up on trying to open his eyes.

Though the pain was still intense in certain places, most of his body felt numb. Of course, that made sense, considering the majority of his nerves would have been burnt to cinders. No, the pain would come later...as his body continued the process of regeneration.

"Just a moment," Daniel said. "First, let us see if we can get some water down that throat of yours."

King felt a small trickle of something cool and wet slap against his lips. He imagined the old man hovering over him, wringing a wet cloth to allow the water to drip into his partially opened mouth.

After a few seconds of the cool relief, he heard the old man sigh. "That should help some," he said. "But then, in all my years, I have never seen anyone quite like you before, have I? I believed you were dead when I found the pyre. I mean, in my visions of you, I had seen you die—a number of times, in fact—and seen you come back to life, though I never imagined that to be taken literally. As I approached the fire though, I heard your screams." He chuckled, but there was no mirth in it. "Imagine my surprise when I reached in and pulled out your severed head...your mouth still open and still silently screaming like a lost soul in the pit of Sheol.

"I managed to get the rest of you out of the blaze, and the strangest thing started happening..."

King didn't need to listen to what happened next. He knew all too well. His head and torso had been placed close enough together that tissue, veins, arteries and tendons would have begun to grow. They would have extended out, sweeping the ground like unholy tentacles searching for their mates. Eventually, these tendrils would have connected. Bonded. Then, they would have retracted, pulling King's head toward its proper place, where the rest of his body would begin the arduous process of knitting it back together. He'd seen his teammate, Bishop, go through similar trauma before. He knew all too well what the old prophet would have seen.

The fact that Daniel hadn't thrown him right back into the fire for possessing demonic powers was a testament to the man's wisdom. Or, at the very least, his mercy. King wasn't sure how he would have responded to such a horror, if the roles had been reversed.

"...so, as I said, I am a little out of my realm of knowledge here, but your body does seem to be healing. Rather rapidly too. Those fingers I told you about? I can already see new ones forming. Your right arm has grown nearly two inches since I mentioned it. Patches of skin are flaking away to reveal new, raw flesh underneath. If I had to guess, I would say you will be back as good as new by this time tomorrow."

Once again, King attempted to open his eyes. This time, the resistance was minimal, and he managed to peer through tiny slits to see a blurry vision of the old man huddled beside him. Concern was etched on the prophet's face, but his eyes betrayed a sense of wonder and hope.

King looked around. From what he could see through his horribly dehydrated eyes, they were in a cave. A campfire burned in the center of the chamber, illuminating the space with a warm, orange light.

"D-don't have a d-day," King rasped. "The prince n-needs me."

"The prince will be fine for the time being," Daniel said. "The journey to Eridu on foot is another five days march. Sereb-Meloch will not harm the boy until they get to the tomb. And I have horses. They can get you there in under three days. You need to rest now. Let your body do whatever magic it does to make you well."

Daniel reached down, dipped a cloth into a hollowed out piece of tree bark filled with water, and brought the rag up to King's lips. "Here, have some more." King parted his lips a little farther apart and allowed a few moist drops of heaven to glide down his throat. "Now rest. Let your body heal. We will be on the road to help our young charge this time tomorrow."

King wanted to protest. Wanted to argue. But his body refused to cooperate. It demanded sleep, and there was nothing he could do to deny it that. Soon, after tasting a few more drops of the cool water, he let himself slip off into a dreamless sleep.

17

When King awoke the next day, his body was almost entirely regenerated. *Well, perhaps that's not the best word*, he thought. More like mobile. Useable. He still wasn't entirely sure how the healing process worked or why it took longer for some injuries to repair than others. Daniel had insisted that the healing had accelerated even more than normal, because the prophet had spent the entire night in earnest prayer over him. King wasn't entirely sure that was true, but he couldn't argue with the results.

He stood by his horse, packing their meager supplies in a leather bag, which he then slung over the nag. His skin was still pretty charred. Blackened. Though flakes of ash and soot continued to crumble away with every movement to reveal tender, fresh skin beneath. He had no idea what his face looked like, but he could imagine it would have been striking to anyone who saw him.

"What is your plan?" Daniel asked, handing him a bladder of water for the journey.

"Ride as fast and as hard as she'll carry me." King nodded to the horse. "Then get the prince out of harm's way and bring down the wrath of God on Sereb-Meloch's head."

King ground his brittle, charred teeth at the mention of the name. Yes, he'd been through a lot in the two hundred years he'd lived in the past. He'd suffered plenty of injuries. Plenty of deaths. But none had been quite like this. Immolation was a horrible way to be killed, especially when you don't die easily. He wasn't certain it was an experience he could just brush aside like he'd done in the past. It would stay with him. Haunt his dreams. Scar his psyche in ways he couldn't possibly imagine. And although there was nothing he could do about that, he could certainly keep his promise to the damned high priest. He'd be sure the bastard knew exactly what King had endured by his hand.

"May I present to you another option?" Daniel asked.

King turned to him, convinced he didn't want to hear this alternative. If it kept him one second longer from saving the boy and exacting his revenge against the priest, he was certain of it. But one look in the old man's determined eyes told him he should listen.

Daniel held out his hand. He was holding an object wrapped in an ash-covered cloth. King took it and peeled back the rag to reveal a strange, round disc about three inches in diameter and a quarter of an inch thick. The disc looked golden at first, but as he moved it in the light of the sun, it changed colors: gold, green, blue, yellow, red and a mixture of them all, depending on where the light hit it. If King didn't know better, he'd almost believe the metal of the disc was holographic, though there was no discernable image on its surface as far as he could tell. The metal it was made of was also completely foreign to him. King was no metallurgist, but he was certain the material wasn't made of any naturally occurring substance. He wasn't even sure it was made from anything on earth.

"This is what the Girtablilu gave me just before..." King trailed off, reluctant to relive the experience of the past twenty-four hours. Instead, he held the disc up into the light. There was some sort of strange writing on it, but the language was unfamiliar to him as well. "What is it?"

The old man shrugged. "I am uncertain. But I believe it is important. There was a reason those creatures wanted you to have it." Daniel held out his hand, silently asking for the disc back. When King complied, the old prophet looked up at him with deep, sad eyes. "There is more to the Girtablilu than anyone knows. A story of slavery and despair. I believe I am one of the few who know of it, and that is only because it was revealed to me in a dream I had years ago, when an Assyrian general threatened Babylon.

"I will not go into the specifics of the dream, because it was pertinent to political matters at the time, but there was one portion that was completely out of place with the rest, as if Yahweh-Yireh had placed it there solely for my benefit. Solely for a time such as this." He paused as he examined the metal piece more closely. "I had not thought of it in years, but this medallion reminded me of the dream. I saw a great star falling from the sky and crashing into the earth. The star, I have surmised, was the goddess Tiamat. That much was clear to me. What I could not understand at the time, however, was how there could be creatures living inside this goddess...slaves and masters, priests of Tiamat, all working daily to keep her aloft in the Sea of the Void, which hovers above us all."

"Space. You're talking about space."

The old man shrugged. "I suppose. But Tiamat was seen, by those who believe in such tales, as the god of the primordial salt waters that existed before all of creation. These salt waters were in the firmament. Space, as you call it." He paused to gather his thoughts, then continued on with the events of the dream. "When Tiamat fell to the earth, she crashed into Apsu and the two became entwined in carnal passion."

"Apsu?" King asked. There was something about the name in his studies, something that disturbed him. But he couldn't quite place it.

"Apsu was the god of fresh water. The goddess of salt water and the god of fresh, co-mingling together in perfect harmony. The myth goes on to say that this, in fact, was how all life came into existence."

"Apsu... Apsu... Wait, is that the same thing as Abzu? The mystical waters said to flow in underground aquifers under..."

"Under the ziggurat at Eridu. Precisely."

King stood dumbfounded. "Sonuva..."

Now he knew exactly where he'd heard the word before...as well as where he'd heard of the city of Eridu. It had come up during the research for one of Chess Team's missions. They'd been searching for the place where all language on earth was said to have originated. The Tower of Babel. And although that mission had eventually led to Turkey, Eridu and Abzu were names he had come across.

If Daniel noticed King's obvious consternation, he didn't act on it. Instead, he continued with his narrative unperturbed. "After the great beast had copulated with Apsu, I saw the surrounding landscape do the strangest things. The air became unbreathable. Green-tinted vapor arose from the earth, smothering everything for miles. Plants and animals withered and died. In their place, new kinds of vegetation bloomed, but soon, they too, perished and the desert overtook everything.

"Soon, men came to where the great goddess lay within the marshy arms of her lover. She was barely breathing at this point, and in agony. The vapors had all but dissipated and the creatures living inside her were weakened by her impending demise. Most were slaughtered by the invading men. In my dream, I saw a handful of the creatures surviving. They fled deeper into the safety of the goddess's womb, to a place inaccessible to their attackers. They sealed themselves in the very bowels of the great beast, protected by great crystals of ice. In essence, they cut themselves off from their comrades and the rest of the world. Those of their kind not fast enough or wise enough to follow, perished a most gruesome death. Even their priestly masters, with all their great might, had been too weakened by the crash to offer much resistance. Like you, they had been resilient in the best of times—difficult to kill—but without the breath of their goddess to sustain them, they all fell by the swords of men."

King stared at the old man, waiting impatiently for him to get to his point. But when Daniel spoke no further, he arched an eyebrow. "Well?"

"Well what?"

"What does that have to do with me? What's the point of all this?"

The old man lifted the medallion into the air. "This," he said quietly, almost reverently. "I saw the creatures use a medallion just like this to seal themselves into Tiamat's bowels. Those creatures were the same as Tiamba and Namtar. In my dream, they had been enslaved. Forced to labor, day and night, on behalf of the goddess and her strange, demonic priests. They rebelled against their masters, and it was their rebellion that had forced the goddess to fall from the salt void."

King recalled Sereb-Meloch's reference to the Girtablilus' rebellion and his later comment about King being their last hope. *But what does that all mean?* It still didn't explain their knowledge of his callsign, or why they'd given him the medallion in the first place.

He pondered Daniel's dream silently. If he understood what the prophet was saying, Tiamat hadn't been a goddess at all, but rather some sort of spacecraft that had crashed to earth nearly three thousand years before. The Girtablilu had been a slave race, forced to work by another species of aliens.

He couldn't help chuckling in spite of the dire situation. Back in his own time, before joining Chess Team, he would have found such a tale ludicrous. Now, it just seemed like another day at the office.

"So why do you think Tiamba gave me this medallion? What does it have to do with me or my plans for Sereb-Meloch?"

Daniel was prepared for the question. "Because I think the prince's instincts were correct from the start. I think it is essential that you get to Tiamat's tomb before the blasphemer and his army," he said. "Despite your skill and your unearthly abilities, Sereb-Meloch's forces far exceed anything you are capable of doing alone. You have his mercenary army to contend with. His personal guard of warrior-priests. And, though I am not sure how he is controlling them, Tiamba and Namtar. You can attack them day after day...die a thousand deaths for the next thousand years...and never overtake them. What you need is your *own* army."

"Now that you've told me what all this is about, I'm not sure I understand why it's so important." King paused. "From what you've described of your dream, Tiamat isn't a creature that *can* be resurrected. She's not a goddess or a demon or even a beast. She's a spaceship...er, a vessel used to travel the, um, salt void, as you call it. So what's the big deal if he ends up opening the tomb? He'd never know how to operate the damn thing. Why not rush in, grab the kid and run? What would really happen if he succeeds?"

If King's revelation regarding Tiamat's nature was a surprise to the old man, he didn't show it. Instead, he simply nodded his understanding, bent down and plucked a small desert plant from its root. "Because of this, King. Because of this plant. The dirt. The air all around us. Should Sereb-Meloch succeed in awakening Tiamat... Well, do you remember what I said happened to the land surrounding her body once she fell from the sky?"

"The indigenous plant and animal life died. They were replaced by new species of... Oh, God." King understood everything. Well, almost everything—he still didn't get his relationship to the scorpion men—but he now knew enough to comprehend the complete and utter devastation that would occur if the mad man succeeded in his quest.

"Do you think Sereb-Meloch knows?" King asked. "I mean, the truth behind just what Tiamat really is? The power she possesses?"

Daniel nodded. "I have no doubt," he said, handing the metallic disc back to King. "The army of men that destroyed the demon creatures residing in Tiamat's belly was led by one man. A brilliant king. A philosopher, a great hunter and a world renowned scientist."

"Let me take a wild guess and say it was Nimrod."

"Exactly. But what you may not know is that many believe he is the basis for the legend of Marduk, the god who is said to have killed Tiamat to begin with. After his conquest, Nimrod constructed a great pyramid on the remains of the dead goddess, and then he built the city of Eridu around the pyramid. Once construction was complete and Eridu the city of his dreams, Nimrod closed the tomb, using his own blood, mixed with a magical incantation to seal it off from the rest of the world forever."

"Which is why Sereb-Meloch needs Belshazzar," King added. "If his royal ancestry goes back that far, then he's Nimrod's descendent, and therefore carries the same DNA...er, he's of the same bloodline. His blood should be a close enough match to open the sealed tomb."

"Yes," the old man said, "but here is how I suspect the high priest knows the secret of Tiamat's tomb. Why his aspirations are so dangerous. For nearly two decades, Sereb-Meloch served as one of Nebuchadnezzar's chief magi. The official keeper of the kingdom's arcane secrets. Some of those secrets, I later discovered after his banishment, included several very rare artifacts handed down from Nimrod himself. These artifacts were obviously of unearthly origin. Demonic at their very core. Though, thankfully, dormant. But among these artifacts were several tablets containing detailed accounts of tales passed down by Nimrod. They regarded his encounter with the dying Tiamat and her children, as the creatures inside her womb came to be called. When I began cataloging these tablets, as well as the arcane trinkets and talismans within the collection, I discovered a few were missing. When banished from the Kingdom, Sereb-Meloch must have taken the objects and documents most important to his goal. I have no idea what these tablets said, but I daresay they revealed the dark secrets that lay within Tiamat's resting place."

"Which is why I need to get to the temple at Eridu before he does," King said, swinging himself onto the back of his horse with a grace that belied his fire-scarred body. The pain was intense, but bearable for the moment. He tucked the strange disc in the pouch at his belt and looked down at Daniel.

"Anything else I need to know, old man?"

"Just two more things," he answered. "First, I will be following as soon as I can. I am not sure what these old bones can do to help you, but my prayers are strong, and I do have a few tricks I have learned over the years that might assist."

"And the second thing?"

The old man chuckled. A glint twinkled in his eyes as he smiled up at King. "I will tell you the second thing when all of this is over."

King smiled back at him and nodded. "Fair enough." He then spurred the horse forward and bolted toward the decaying city of Eridu and a goddess's tomb.

18

Wasteland, Southwest of Uruk

King drove the horse as hard as he dared. Though dangerous in the deep sand of the desert, they rode on through the night and on until the afternoon of the next day. Sereb-Meloch and his crew had a full day and a half head start. But as Daniel had pointed out, the majority of his army was on foot. Belshazzar was in a rickety, mule-driven cart. The going would be slow.

Though every fiber of his being wanted to forget about Eridu and go directly to save the kid, King knew it would be a mistake. He'd sworn an oath to protect the prince, but if what the prophet had told him was even half true, there was too much at stake. Tiamat's high priest could not be allowed to enter the tomb. Could not be allowed to revive her.

King knew what the Tiamat ship was, what it was designed to do. The realization of just how close the world had come to obliteration thousands of years ago sent chills down his spine. The clue had been the plant and animal life. The reference to the 'last breath' of the ship and the remaining Girtablilu descending deep into its protective womb just added to his certainty. He knew precisely what Tiamat was capable of, and the legends of its ability to unmake all of creation could not have been more accurate.

Of course, he was taking the word of a man who could very well be completely out of his gourd, but he didn't think so. It was *the* Daniel, after all. One of the greatest prophets of the Old Testament, if one believed in that sort of thing. Though his rational mind rebelled against it, after meeting the man himself, there was little room for any doubt. Daniel knew what he was talking about, and that meant King had to trust what he'd heard.

He shuddered with another chill, pulled his steed to a halt and wrapped his cloak and turban more securely around himself. His skin had nearly completely healed, though he still had patches of bark-like charring over half of his face and his entire left side. What made things worse was that his nerves were beginning to grow back, making every movement, every gentle breeze against his skin, sheer agony. But agony was good. It meant he was alive. Meant he was getting better. Stronger. More capable of unleashing hell on the man who had done this to him.

King ground his teeth at the thought, before kicking his horse into action again and toward his destiny.

The sun was setting on the following day. King adjusted his position on the mare's back. Since saddles as King knew them hadn't been invented yet, staying comfortable during a non-stop ride like this had not been the easiest task. He now added a bruised tail bone to go along with all his other healing injuries, and it annoyed him.

The view just over the ridge on which he and the horse now stood, however, was enough to further sour his dark mood. A mile away, Sereb-Meloch's men busied themselves setting up camp for the night. The sheer number of mercenaries that were now encamped was impressive. The last he'd seen of the high priest's forces, they were no more than one hundred and fifty men. Now, looking down in the shadowy camp, he estimated a group of nearly five hundred.

Sereb-Meloch had picked up reinforcements somewhere along the way.

But why? King wondered. *The only opposition they faced was from me, and they think I'm dead. This many soldiers is overkill.*

As he scanned the camp, his eyes came to a sudden stop, and a wave of relief washed over him. Though he had nowhere near the vision of his friend and teammate, Knight, he could see enough in the dwindling light to ease his mind, at least a little bit, about his predicament. Belshazzar rested, in the confines of the wooden cage. From this distance, it was difficult to be sure, but he appeared unharmed. The two Girtablilu stood at opposite corners of the cage, guarding the boy from any attempts at rescue, King assumed. At that very moment, one of Zaidu's mercenaries tossed a bowl full of slop through the cage bars. Not very appetizing to be sure, but at least they were both feeding and hydrating the boy. Keeping him as healthy as possible until they made it to their destination.

At the rate the processional was traveling, they'd probably arrive in Eridu sometime mid-afternoon the following day, depending on what time they broke camp in the morning. He wasn't sure why the priest wasn't demanding they push on through the night, but he surmised that such a nocturnal trek would prove—

A sudden thought struck King like a Mack truck. The Girtablilu. It had been two days since King had been beheaded and set on fire. And now, though the sun was indeed setting, they were out in the open...had obviously been traveling throughout the day. But when Sereb-Meloch had impatiently worked to release the two from their cavernous prison inside Mount Mashu, he'd insisted that they could not be released during the day. He'd implied the creatures were nocturnal in nature.

So what's changed? Are they nocturnal or aren't they?

King wondered whether it even mattered, but something in the back of his mind told him it most certainly did. Sereb-Meloch had somehow managed to gain complete control over two alien creatures with a track record for rebellion. The question was, how? And did the time of day have anything at all to do with this control? Could King somehow use the answer as a means of undoing the high priest's machinations?

He decided it was worth filing away for a later time. For now, if he wanted to beat his enemies to the prize, he needed to leave. With any luck, he could be there by morning.

19

Ruined City of Eridu

The sun had been up for less than three hours and already the air around King felt like the inside of a brick pizza oven. To make matters worse, it wasn't the typical dry furnace of the desert, but a drenching tropical heat from the nearby marshy land in the valley below—the valley containing the sand-swept remains of a nearly forgotten city: Eridu.

Climbing down from his horse, he edged up to the nearby ridge and glanced down at the vast wasteland below. The ancient city—by all accounts, one of the very first cities ever constructed—was barely visible now. The walls, once a great barrier against invading hordes, lay in piles of rubble and debris. Buildings, temples and homes were little more than sand mounds, dotting the terrain. Little else of the old metropolis could be discerned among the sand and swamp land, except for the peak of a massive step-pyramid that lay dormant on the far end of the city.

King knew from his studies that the place wouldn't be fully excavated until sometime in the late nineteenth century. So why, he wondered, was there a full regiment of soldiers, workers, servants and engineers currently surrounding the ziggurat? Why had four hastily-constructed watchtowers been erected on each side of the city? And why were teams of slaves digging furiously to uncover the entrance to the temple?

Of course, he already knew the answer. The multi-colored standards that flapped in the marshland's fetid breeze told him as much. Nebuchadnezzar had sent in his troops to prevent Sereb-Meloch's forces from entering the Tomb of Tiamat.

Now King understood the unexpected reinforcements within Sereb-Meloch's camp. His scouts must have discovered that the Babylonian ruler had stationed troops in Eridu, and he'd been recruiting soldiers ever since.

At first, King was elated at the revelation. He now would have help in his mission. Backup. A full battalion of nearly four hundred well-trained and heavily armored Babylonian soldiers could effectively crush the high priest's horde of mercenaries, cutthroats, warrior-priests and even the two Girtablilu. Granted, Sereb-Meloch still outnumbered them slightly, but King had no doubt that Nebuchadnezzar's forces could easily outmatch the others in terms of skill and weaponry.

King scrambled closer to the edge and lay flat on his belly to watch the ant-like workers clearing away the sand and rubble around the pyramid. *What are they doing?* If they wanted to keep the high priest out, why would they be clearing the doorway for him? Why make it easier for the madman to reach his goal?

Then, three separate thoughts struck King at once. First, he would find no support from the mad king's men.

Second, they no longer had orders to kill the prince. King was sure of that. The third thought explained the second— somehow, Nebuchadnezzar had discovered the secret of the Eridu pyramid and the earth-shattering technology that lay within. He wanted it for himself, and they would need the boy for the same reasons as Sereb-Meloch.

Granted, the theory was a stretch, but it made sense. Yes, Nebuchadnezzar could conceivably open the door with his own DNA. After all, he was theoretically a descendent of Nimrod as well. However, the Babylonian ruler would undoubtedly see the risks as too great. No telling what horrors might be awakened once the spacecraft's doors were finally opened. King doubted the man would want to be within a hundred miles of the place when that happened. So, who better to use than an heir already marked for death?

The burn scars across King's body itched as his veins filled with vitriol for Belshazzar's dear old grandfather. It was bad enough when he'd issued the decree to have the boy killed. Now, he could very well be intending to use him as a guinea pig. King seethed at the very thought.

"That's not gonna happen," he mumbled to himself, as he wrapped his tagelmust around his face. Leaving his horse alone on the ridge, he crept down the embankment to the valley below and mapped out his plan.

20

After slipping past the westernmost watchtower, King dipped into some nearby underbrush and waited until dark. Once the sun had set, he clung to the shadows and crept into the interior of the decaying city.

The soldiers' vigilance was pitiful to say the least. Whether because they were expecting an army of cutthroats to come barreling over the northwest ridge like a stampede of elephants or just from overconfidence, King had no problem navigating the darkened, sand-covered streets. Of course, with the tagelmust wrapped securely over his face and head, and the dark brown linen of his robes, he blended in perfectly with the night. Even the most wary guards would have had a difficult time spotting him, and by the time they had, he would have already been close enough to disable them before they could so much as utter a word.

King hoped it wouldn't come to that. Much better for all involved if he could reach the temple's entrance without encountering any opposition at all. He knew that once he engaged the first combatant, it would be that much more difficult to keep his presence in Eridu a secret.

Darting between two dilapidated buildings, he waited as a squad of soldiers passed. He then snaked his way to within a hundred yards of where the slaves chipped away at the centuries of sand and detritus that had blocked the entry of the tomb. At the rate they were going, the path would most likely be cleared by around noon the following day. That was too long for King to wait to get inside and too soon for him to be confident he could prevent anyone else getting in.

He needed to consider an alternative. Demolish the entire site? He couldn't see that happening. Though he'd managed to whip up his own homemade batch of plastique, it wasn't nearly potent enough to destroy an entire archaeological site, and Alfred Nobel wasn't scheduled to invent dynamite for another few thousand years or so.

Okay, then what other options do I have?

He glanced around for ideas. Another watchtower lay just two hundred yards to the north. A perfect vantage point to see something he'd missed along the ridge or as he'd skulked through the town. From what he could see, there was only one soldier keeping watch on the thirty foot platform. Easy enough to take out clandestinely.

King snuck around the eastern face of the pyramid, avoiding the line of sight of both the slaves and their drivers, and headed north.

Around the mid-point of the temple, he was brought to an abrupt halt when a tremor erupted from somewhere inside his robes. Startled, he fumbled at the robe's folds until he reached the inner pocket that held the medallion. He pulled it out to discover the strange disc was vibrating madly and emitting a dim, green glow around its edges.

Okay. What set you off, I wonder.

He turned around from the direction he'd just come and the vibrations slackened. He headed north once more and the disc became even more kinetic than before.

Some kind of homing mechanism? he thought. *But to what?*

His best guess—or perhaps it was nothing more than a vague hope—was that it was pointing him in the direction of another entrance. If the medallion acted as some sort of magnetic keycard, as Daniel had seemed to indicate based on his dreams, then perhaps it had detected the nearby presence of a receptor into which it fit.

He turned to face the ziggurat. He scanned the exposed surface of the temple's peak, searching for anything that might be used as a door. There was no telling where it might be located. More than three-fourths of the structure was buried in sand and muck. If another door existed, it could be buried more than seventy-five feet deep. It might take weeks to uncover.

King froze at a sudden noise from around the northeast corner. Two men talking. Possibly a patrol making their regular rounds along the temple grounds. He glanced around, looking for a place to hide, but he found nothing but open space, the wall to the ziggurat's apex and two nearby palm trees.

"Well, shit," he mumbled just as the two guards came into view. From this distance, King was still relatively shrouded in darkness. He wouldn't be easily detected for another twenty yards or so. And then, all bets would be off. With no long range weapons, taking out two well-trained soldiers silently was going to be tricky.

He crouched down, obscuring himself even further in the shadows, pulled a dagger from his sash, which Daniel had provided him, and counted down each guard's steps.

The soldiers' armor clanked noisily with each footfall. One carried a spear, perched casually on his shoulder. The other, a short sword.

When they were no more than fifty yards away, the spear-wielder stopped suddenly.

"Just a second," he said to his companion.

King froze.

The second guard turned to look at his partner. "What is it? What's wrong?"

The first man bent over and fiddled with something around his feet. He then stood up, used the spear shaft as a balance and raised his foot into the air before shaking it. "I've got something in my boot," he said. "A rock, I think. It's been bothering me all night."

King let out his breath with a smile. *Ah, the joys of perimeter duty*, he thought, remembering his early years in the military. No matter which era one lived in, some things never changed.

After a few minutes, the guard brought his foot down once more, gave the ground a quick stomp, and sighed with relief. "Ah, much better!" He adjusted his bullet-shaped helmet and nodded to the other soldier.

But King was no longer paying attention. Something had caught his attention the moment the guard had stomped his foot. A faint, subtle sound of metal underneath the sand. Metal...on a stone pyramid? King knew he'd just found the hidden entrance for which he'd been searching. All that remained was to deal with the two soldiers before they could raise an alarm.

He watched as the two men chatted, reluctant to resume their patrol. King could relate. He'd spent many hours on sentry duty himself, wiling away the long, tedious hours with little to do. He recalled just how much relief it had been to connect with another living soul during those times. To speak to another human being in the darkest hours before dawn. These Babylonian soldiers were little different than the buddies he'd made while in the Army, before being chosen for Delta.

"...and I couldn't believe what she said to her husband when it was all over," laughed the spear guy. "It was madness, I tell you."

"Well," said the other. "What did she say?"

King ignored the conversation. Now, while they were distracted, was the time to act.

He snuck forward, crab-walking toward them like a great spider along its web. He'd easily broken the twenty yard boundary, and they'd still not seen him. If he could just make it a few more yards, he'd be able to take the two guards out silently and possibly avoid killing them. All he needed was a little luck and...

The soldier on King's right turned to face him, just as he reached striking distance.

As understanding dawned on the soldier's face, his mouth opened to shout, but King struck too quickly. Pushing off with his legs, he bolted upright, his right fist plowing into the man's jaw. The soldier collapsed to the ground just as his partner spun around, a spear twirling over his head in preparation for battle. The spear shot forward and would have pierced King's left thigh, if he hadn't swiveled to his right at the last second.

Unfazed by King's speed, the soldier brought the spear around and slammed the shaft down on King's shoulder. King stumbled forward from the blow, but did not fall. Instead, he used the momentum in a forward roll and came up behind the spear-wielder, reached around his head and with a quick jerk, snapped the man's neck. The subsequent crack of the spine frustrated King. He'd felt a certain camaraderie with the man and his fellow soldier. But King's mission was paramount, and he had to remind himself that these men would not have hesitated to kill him if given the chance. Worse, they could have possibly set their sights on Belshazzar.

Quietly, he lowered the dead man to the ground and set to work on binding his unconscious partner with leather straps. Once the man was secured and gagged, King scrambled over to the patch of ground from which he'd noticed the metallic sound. After a quick two minute search, he found it. Digging furiously with his hands, King wiped away the sand until he'd uncovered a strange metal access port embedded in one of the stone steps of the ziggurat. The hatch, similar to the metal used in the medallion, was perfectly round and nearly two feet in diameter.

King's hand felt around the port, searching for a latch or slot in which to insert his disc, but he couldn't find anything. As a matter of fact, the hatch was so flush with the stone, he couldn't even locate a seam or hinge to allow it to open.

"Okay..." he whispered aloud. "So what am I doing wrong here?" Curious, he pulled out the medallion and felt it vibrate in the palm of his hand. Oddly, the disc's tremors had reached a certain frequency and now remained fixed, as he held over the portal. "What exactly am I supposed to do?"

He set the medallion down next to the circle of metal on the ground and allowed himself a moment to think the process through. He'd expected to find a control panel or scanner or something to unlock the door, but if such a device was there, it was still hidden by centuries of sand.

Or, he thought, *it's something outside the box. Something outside of my own experience.*

He picked up the disc again and examined the metal more closely. Once, twice, even three times, he compared the strange holographic material to that of the access port. To the naked eye, they were absolutely identical.

Curiously, he placed the disc on top of the hatch. Immediately, it burst into a bright green glow, followed by a rushing hiss. King watched amazed as both portal and key shimmered into a strange, opaque liquid. The substance resembled molten ore, yet radiated no heat.

Well, this is new.

He took the dead man's spear and stuck it through the liquid. It passed with no resistance. When he yanked it out, the tip and shaft appeared completely undamaged.

Still wary, he searched his immediate space and discovered a small stone. Holding it a few inches from the gelatin-like surface, he dropped it through the portal. It, too, passed without any issues, though to be fair, he had no idea what had happened to it on the other side.

A low moan from behind swept King's attention away from the portal. The remaining soldier was coming to. Granted, he was tied up, and the gag would prevent him from alerting his comrades, but King couldn't take any chances. He reached into the pouch tied to his belt, and withdrew a mixture of herbs he'd discovered in his two-hundred year sojourn. Crushing them with the palm of his hand, he slipped over to the prostrate man and poured the dry contents down the groggy man's throat and waited. Within seconds, the man was unconscious again. Grabbing the soldier's sword and tucking it into his belt, King quickly returned to the portal with a fresh idea.

Organic, he thought. *A spear and a pebble is one thing. Flesh is something altogether different.*

He glanced at the dead soldier to his left, then eyed the pulsing liquid. He returned to the man he had killed and shrugged. He dragged the corpse to the lip of the hole. Slowly, he dipped the soldier's hand into the liquid and immediately withdrew it. Nothing.

Confident he'd tested it as much as he could, King took a deep breath and plunged his own arm into the viscous metallic liquid. Though he felt an odd tingling sensation in his limb, there was no pain. Nothing uncomfortable. When he withdrew it and saw that he was still intact, he tossed the spear completely through the opening and followed immediately after it, into the unknown.

21

King dropped to the floor. When he looked up at the ceiling, the portal was nowhere to be seen. A quick search around him in the near-dark chamber revealed that the circular pool of liquid was now on the wall to his left.

But that's not possible... unless...

He let his train of thought loose for a few moments to hypothesize the displaced access port. If he was indeed standing in the bowels of some deep-space vessel and if it had crashed, there was a good chance it hadn't landed right-side up. He thought that a deep-space craft might utilize some form of artificial gravity that would attempt, if sustained with enough energy, to keep the ship's interior equalized spatially. In other words, if the vessel *did* have artificial gravity, the device might simply orient its interior to the correct position. If he was correct, King hadn't dropped *down* into the ship, but rather simply entered it.

It's as good an explanation as any, he thought, as he turned his attention to more pressing matters like figuring out how to retrieve the medallion from the portal mechanism. If Daniel was correct, then the disc was needed to reach the other Girtablilu, who'd been hiding somewhere in the bowels of the ship. After three thousand years, he would have doubted any of them could have survived, but then he remembered Tiamba and Namtar. Both had survived for that long, locked away in a cavern. If they'd managed it without support or technology of any kind, surely their brethren, confined to the advanced systems of an alien craft, could have as well. But whether they still lived or not would be moot if he couldn't access the doorway.

Instinctively, he reached out to the liquid hatch and hovered his hand near its surface. He wasn't surprised when nothing happened. He then inserted his hand to try to feel around for the disc, but from the warmth on the skin of his hand, he'd simply reached through the portal.

"Well, great," he said, retracting his arm. "All I wanted was the damn key." As if on cue, the liquid solidified into the multi-colored metal once again. The medallion, now fully intact, hovered millimeters away from the portal. *Voice activated* and *it knows English.* He paused, then reached out and plucked the disc from mid-air. "Cool."

The moment the disc was in King's grasp, the chamber echoed with hums and clicks, followed by an ethereal blue glow cast by a train of recessed lights. Once King's eyes adjusted to the sudden glare, he discovered he was standing in a long corridor. The walls and floors of the complex were made of a marble-like black material with veins of gray and white. Their polished surface absorbed the light coming from the elliptical ceiling, reducing the illumination. There weren't any windows, and there was no décor or doorways that he could see in either direction, which stretched on for as far as he could see. The craft—if that was what it was—was much larger than the ruined city above him. From his brief, first glimpse of the ship's interior, it could stretch for miles.

It didn't seem possible. If the purpose of the craft was what he suspected, it should have been built to enter a world's atmosphere with little difficulty. But something this size... It would have been absolutely impossible to hold together in the sky, under the weight of the Earth's gravity. There would be no way the pilots could have possibly hoped to land something this massive on Earth.

So what am I missing? If it's not a spaceship, then what is it?

For the moment, he decided to put the question aside. He had more pressing matters with which to concern himself. Sereb-Meloch's army would reach Eridu sometime later that day—probably afternoon, if his calculations were correct. If King had any chance of stopping both the high priest's and Nebuchadnezzar's' armies, he needed to find the Girtablilu. Of course, if his previous encounters with Tiamba and Namtar were any indication of what was waiting for him, he wasn't certain he wanted their help.

Brushing his trepidation aside, he grasped the medallion in his hand and waited. If the thing had led the way to the interior hatch, it might do the same with other doors. And one of those doors would have to be where the surviving scorpion men had secured themselves. At first, the disc remained dormant. No matter which direction he turned, he could sense no reaction from it at all. He chose a direction at random and began walking.

After the first ten minutes, his brisk walk became a slow trot, as he traversed the never-ending hallway. The trot soon escalated to a jog, and still, the medallion showed no change. He began to wonder if perhaps he'd made the wrong choice. Maybe he should have gone the other way. He slowed his stride as he pondered the need to retrace his steps, but he thought better of it. *Best to proceed until there's no going forward*, he thought morosely.

PLEASE PROCEED.

King stopped. The new thought inside his head hadn't been his own. He'd heard it in his own mental voice—that much was sure—but the words were an intrusion. After living ninety-seven years near Athens and the rest of the time travelling the ancient world around the Mediterranean, he'd long since stopped thinking in English. Greek had become his 'native language' and this particular thought had clearly been in English. He paused, willing the blood rushing through his ears to quiet. Had he imagined it? Had he heard someone speak and somehow confused it with a thought in his own mind?

PLEASE PROCEED.

His internal voice repeated; once again, not of his own choosing. It sounded disjointed, almost scrambled...like the sound of a radio signal that hadn't quite been squelched. Or a mixture of his own voice and that of a Cylon from *Battlestar Galactica*, which he'd watched as a kid. But it sounded weaker.

"...the hell is going on?" he whispered, taking another cautious step forward. He paused, waited a beat, then took another. The foreign thoughts did not return. "Hello?" he asked. His voice reverberated down the endless corridor, but nothing answered back.

Satisfied no one was going to reply, he continued his trek down the corridor. His footfalls were eerily silent as he marched. His thick leather soles inexplicably quiet in a place that in other circumstances should have acted as an echo chamber.

STOP.

The internal voice directed him again. King complied and glanced around. As far as he could tell, the marbled black walls to his right and left were exactly the same as the seeming miles of wall he'd just passed. Furthermore, from what he could tell, the corridor still stretched indefinitely ahead, though he began to detect the slightest trace of a right-hand curve. There was no discernable reason for him to stop at this point.

There was a sudden hiss to his right. He turned his attention in that direction, just in time to see a circlet of the holographic metal materialize directly out of the wall. Playing a hunch, King withdrew his disc and placed it inside the newly revealed ring and was rewarded by a ripple in the wall that shimmered and swirled until another liquid-like doorway formed before his eyes.

Unlike the hatch he'd slipped through on the far side of the pyramid, this was a full-sized door, proportioned perfectly to allow King entry. *Not full-sized*, he thought wryly. *'King-sized' is more like it.*

"So I suppose you expect me to go in there?" King said, pointing to the door. "Just like that? I have no idea what's on the other side...what dangers I could be stepping into...and you just expect me to trust you enough to comply?"

King wasn't certain how he felt about exploring a place that could conjure perfectly customized doors out of solid marble at will. He wasn't overly fond of the idea of blindly running through the high-tech rat maze, whether Daniel thought it was essential or not. After all, now that he was inside, why wasn't he just searching for the device and destroying it before it could be a danger to anyone?

THAT WOULD BE UNWISE.

The voice inside his head was laced with just a hint of a threat. It didn't like his alternative idea.

"Why?" he shouted, unnerved that his voice cast utterly no echo now. "What would happen if I *did* destroy it?"

THAT WOULD BE UNWISE.

King clenched his fists, frustration building. He considered the possibility that he was simply arguing with his own subconscious, but deep down he knew the truth. Something inside this facility had hacked into his brainwaves and was emitting thoughts directly into his mind.

"Enough is enough. This stops now," King growled, before hefting the spear into a defensive posture and stepping through the door.

22

The Ruined City of Eridu, Above Ground

Only a handful of slaves, a single driver and an injured soldier noticed the soft rumble of the earth the moment King entered the liquid door underneath the pyramid. Even fewer noticed the instant drop in temperature by nearly ten degrees or the panicked exodus of birds that fled the safety of their perches to parts unknown.

The slow-moving plumes of greenish-blue gas that seeped casually up from the sand in various places throughout the desolate city had been noticed only by one soldier, who had wandered off to a secluded spot to relieve himself. As he stood there, looking down at his business, the puffs of the strange vapor had drifted up. He'd stopped immediately, repelled by the putrid stench. He had turned to report the strange occurrence to his superiors, but the words never escaped his lips. He'd collapsed to the ground within seconds, seized by a hacking cough. He'd wheezed pitifully for breath that would never come and eventually perished.

That was five hours ago, and his body had yet to be discovered. Even if it had been, no one would have paid it much mind. It would have simply been one more body among many in the midst of the violent struggle that now raged in the Eridu valley.

King's estimate of Sereb-Meloch's arrival had been wrong. They had arrived just before dawn with a great shout and a blaring of trumpets that rallied the warriors to battle. They'd attacked without warning, dispatching Nebuchadnezzar's scouts before the men could report back of the oncoming army and the two nightmare creatures under their control. Though Nebuchadnezzar's forces had the superior skill and weaponry, they were overwhelmingly outnumbered. With the aid of the Girtablilu, they were also hopelessly outmatched.

So no one noticed as the winds whipped up. Fewer still cared about the sudden electrical storm that sizzled the air with the smell of ozone. There was a battle to be won and no one on either side suspected that the earth itself would bring about their doom.

No one, that is, except for the cloaked, bent form of an old man who had walked two horses casually through the field of battle as if on a noonday stroll.

23

King stepped into some sort of laboratory space. The black-gray marble walls had given way to the stark contrast of antiseptic white. The walls, floor and ceiling were all made of the same foreign material. The lights still pulsed with the same soft blue glow, though its source was not as evident as it had been out in the corridor.

Spear still in hand, King glanced around the room, ready for any surprises that might be lurking nearby.

Finding nothing, he reached out toward the metal circlet beside the door and willed the disc to return. It complied immediately, and the liquid portal solidified once more into a wall. Pocketing the disc, he turned to survey the room more closely. Like everything else he'd encountered since entering the facility—he was still reluctant to call it a ship—the chamber was massive, appearing to be two hundred feet square with a twenty foot high ceiling. The wall space around the entire room was bare. No shelving, tables, or work areas of any kind. But the center of the lab...

King gawked at the enormous glass tubes that covered most of the room. They were well over five foot in diameter and reached from floor to ceiling. Filled with some thick, clear liquid, each of the tubes contained shapes. Creatures of varying size and morphology floated inside each of them. A few—nearly two dozen by King's count—were very familiar to him. The Girtablilu. The others were completely alien to him.

They look like some sort of stasis chambers. Cryogenics or some other form of suspended animation, he thought, as he made his way through the maze of tubes, slowly processing all he was seeing. As he passed each tube, a flicker of light would catch his eye, resolving into a holographic screen displaying what he guessed were the occupant's vital signs, EKGs and other statistical data. He gawked at one tube after another, trying to make sense of the data. Many of the creatures appeared to be dead, their remains preserved forever within the viscous substance encasing them. Of the twenty-four creatures that resembled Tiamba and Namtar, sixteen remained alive. The ratio proved true for the other species confined to the tubes. Close to half were dead.

King rounded a table to discover a stasis chamber unlike all the rest. Instead of standing upright, this one hovered horizontally, two and a half feet off the floor. It wasn't made of glass either, but appeared to be constructed of the same holographic-like metal of the disc and door-locking mechanisms. It looked more like a streamlined sensory deprivation chamber. *Or a space coffin*, he thought.

A few other space coffins were scattered around this section of the lab, but from his vantage point, they all appeared to live up to King's pet name for them. They had all flatlined. Only the holographic readout on the unit directly in front of him pulsed with activity.

He stood his ground, nearly three feet away from this new discovery. Something about it didn't sit right with him. There was something...

APPROACH.

The mechanical echo of his internal voice reverberated inside his head. King suspected that whatever lay inside the horizontal tube was what had been invading his mind. And he didn't like it one bit.

"I don't think so," King said, raising his spear defensively.

APPROACH.

He turned to the tubes containing the Girtablilu, determined to stay on task. The scorpion men were why he'd come...to raise an army. Daniel had inexplicably believed they would assist him, and King couldn't help but trust the man, based on Daniel's legendary reputation alone. Who was he to question a prophet of God?

Shaking his head, he returned to the nearest creature resembling Tiamba and examined the holographic screen in more detail. In his time, he'd seen his share of bio-medical readouts. Had a fair understanding of what most of the jagged and wiggly lines streaking across represented. Heart rate. Oxygen levels...well, maybe not oxygen, but whatever particular gas this species needed to nourish the brain. He read, and comprehended most of the data, but the line he'd believed to be the EEG readout was beyond anything he'd seen before.

The EEG showed enhanced cerebral activity. Even stranger, the creature's gamma wave, normally used to process multiple stimuli simultaneously, was off the charts. This should have been impossible, given that the subject appeared to be unconscious and in a state of suspended animation. For the gamma waves to be so active, the creature would not only need to be conscious, but in a highly agitated state with loads of stimuli coming at it in rapid succession.

As he glanced around from one suspension tube to the next, he discovered the EEGs to be one hundred percent identical. Not just similar. Not close. They were completely identical with every spike and dip. If King was reading them correctly, each of the Girtablilu shared the exact same neurological patterns, which could only happen if they were...

A HIVE MIND, said the voice in his head.

King wheeled around to glare at the horizontal tube. "Stay out of my head!" he shouted, but the voice ignored him.

APPROACH.

"And why the hell should I?"

FOR ANSWERS YOU SEEK. KKIIINNNGGG.

It was all he could do to not show surprise at the mention of his callsign. Of course, the Girtablilu apparently knew who he was. And if the Voice was correct, they also shared a hive mind. A collective consciousness. What one of them knew, they apparently all knew. So it shouldn't be any surprise that the Voice knew his name as well. For now, he decided, he wouldn't take the bait. "That's not good enough. I think I'll take my cha..."

THE LAND ABOVE IS ALREADY DYING. A BATTLE RAGES. MY HIGH PRIEST HAS ARRIVED. I WILL SET THE WORLD ABLAZE IF YOU DO NOT APPROACH.

King froze. Sereb-Meloch was already here? How long had he been searching the hallways? And what did the Voice mean by 'the land above is already dying'? More questions, King supposed, that the speaker inside his mind was offering to answer for him—if he complied.

He glanced at the horizontal tube, then back at the Girtablilu.

FORGET MY CHILDREN. THEY CANNOT ASSIST YOU. ONLY I AM CAPABLE OF THAT.

Reluctantly, King stepped forward. "And who, exactly, are you?" he asked, as he slowly approached. The palms of his hands sweated against the smooth wood of the spear.

THE GREAT GODDESS. THE CREATOR OF ALL THAT IS, was its cold reply. *I AM TIAMAT.*

King slammed the spearhead down on the tube, eliciting a raucous echo throughout the lab. "I said stay out of my head!" he growled. Maybe not the wisest move on his part, but certainly satisfying.

"Is this better?" came a disembodied electronic voice. The tinny quality to it enhanced the perception of some type of science fiction android in King's imagination. But it wasn't using his mind this time. He glanced around, but couldn't identify the source.

"Is this better?" the voice repeated.

There is nothing good about me talking to an immortal goddess with the power to create and destroy worlds, he thought. "Yes. As long as you stop manipulating my thoughts, we'll be just fine." He stepped closer to the ten-foot-long, high tech sarcophagus. "Now, for the question we've all been waiting for...aren't you a little short for a Tiamat?" When there was no response to his quip, he added, "Look, what exactly do you want from me?"

There was a squeal of electric static, then the thing calling itself Tiamat spoke. The answer chilled King to the core.

"Freedom."

24

King drew closer to the sarcophagus. He really wished it had been made of glass like the others. His curiosity about the creature inside was getting the better of him. But if the ship harbored the device he believed it did, there was no way he could consider releasing the creature. He let his hand hover over the sarcophagus's surface, sweeping it back and forth as if trying to feel any evil that might emanate from within. Realizing what he was doing—and remembering how the other things in the facility responded to thought or gesture—he pulled his hand back with a snap.

"Answers first," he said, trying to be as non-committal as possible. "How were you projecting your thoughts into my head?"

"Why is that important?"

"Because I'd like to understand it before I do anything. I'd like to know if I can trust my own decisions or if you can compel me to action."

"And you will believe what I tell you?"

That's a good point, he thought.

"You said you'd provide answers. This will be a start in that direction." He also knew he was running out of time. Answers might have to take a backseat. If Tiamat was telling the truth, all hell was breaking loose topside. But obtaining some of his answers might be the first step in figuring out how to stop the device.

"First, place your hand against the widest end of my containment unit," the voice echoed in the chamber.

"Not a chance. Answer the question."

There was a hiss of static, followed by what sounded like a word. King couldn't make out what was said. Finally, it spoke again. "The chamber will not open. It will merely reveal a window through which we can see each other. Much better to communicate face-to-face."

King hesitated. Considered the request, then thought better of it. "Answer my question."

There was another pause, then something that distinctly sounded like a sigh. "Before I answer, let me be clear. I know what you are. I know where you are from. Because of that, I will dispense with treating you the same as I would the primitives of this era."

"Sounds smart," King said. Suddenly, his heart skipped against his chest. The spear was no longer in his hand. He glanced around and found it leaning against the wall, near the closest suspension tube holding one of the scorpion men.

When did I do that? he wondered. But before he had time to contemplate it fully, the creature known as Tiamat spoke again.

"To answer your question," the voice echoed in the chamber, "The Girtablilu communicate by a mixture of body language, pheromones and telepathy. We designed them this way, to be more effective warriors."

Warriors, King thought, realizing the implications. "You have enemies...out there."

"The universe is vast." The Voice paused. "And our race had lost the ability to physically contend with others we encountered, so we engineered a species better suited to combat. To allow instant coordination and strategic implementation, we created them with a hive mind. What one knows, they all know. What one feels, they all feel."

Having suffered enough deaths to feed a small war, King could only imagine the torture such a hive existence would be. When one of them died, they all experienced it. Still, he could understand the wisdom in such an engineering decision, barbaric though it might be.

"Naturally, my species does not communicate the same way," it said. "To issue commands and ensure total control over the Girtablilus, we developed technology to help project our thoughts to them...to help guide them."

"That's where I have a problem," King said. It was nearly a growl. "*Control.*"

"These are not sentient beings as you know them, Jack Sigler," Tiamat said. "They do not process thought the same as our two species do. They are more primal. More instinctive. The hive mind functions like a genetically coded instructional batch file. They were bred for a specific purpose. They are born fully prepared on a genetic level to fight and obey. Any other thoughts they may have are more akin to emotions. Instincts. Passions. Our mental invasion into their consciousness merely suggests activity direction. We do not impose our will on them. We simply tweak their primitive, baser instincts."

"Their minds may be primitive, but somehow they were able to recognize me. They knew who I was," King argued. "They knew my callsign. They remembered me. How do you explain that?"

"That," the creature paused, as if collecting its thoughts, "is perplexing to me as well. They most definitely knew you, though I've not been able to discern just how. It was their knowledge that allowed me to learn of you as well."

And there it is, King thought. *It just answered my most important questions.* The creature could not only implant its thoughts for communicative purposes, it could control others by inserting suggestions into a target's subconscious. More than that, it could...

YES, JACK SIGLER, the Voice was inside his head again. *THE TECHNOLOGY ALSO ALLOWS ME TO 'READ YOUR THOUGHTS' AS YOU DESCRIBE IT. AMONG A MYRIAD OF OTHER USEFUL THINGS.*

An explosive hiss of air filled the room. Surprised, King jerked back, pulling his hand away from the sarcophagus lid. Sometime during the conversation, completely unaware of what he was doing, he had placed the medallion into a hidden slot and activated the thing's release mechanism.

He'd done it! He'd freed Tiamat! *Sonofabitch.*

25

King leapt away from the thing as the lid's surface melted into the same hazy liquid of the doors he'd stumbled through. An acrid plume of blue-green vapor rushed from the sarcophagus, filling the laboratory with a cloud of unbreathable air.

He winced as he caught a whiff of the stuff. The thing sprayed sulfur into the air. The creature inside breathed sulfur. King had no doubt that's what the terraforming device hidden somewhere in the downed craft—the same device King had come to destroy—was spewing into the air above Eridu.

A sudden thought struck him. *Not a device.* His lungs burned, eliciting a fit of coughs while he put the pieces together. The terraforming machine—technology designed to make an uninhabitable planet into a habitable one—wasn't merely some piece of machinery hidden somewhere onboard. He thought about the never ending corridor, how it seemed to far exceed the dimensions of a craft capable of entering the Earth's gravitational pull. He thought about the liquid metal tech that seemed tantamount to the ship's overall architecture. And everything fell into place. *I'm not looking for a device. It's the entire ship. The ship itself is the terraforming machine.*

The ship was *supposed* to land, and then burrow into the Earth's soil. Once properly positioned, the liquid metal could spread out, creating a subterranean network of tunnels like the roots of some huge, demonic plant. Then, taking the minerals and nutrients from the Earth itself, it could convert all the resources it discovered into a breathable atmosphere for Tiamat's people. To stop it from happening, King was going to have to discover a way to destroy the ship.

His coughing intensified. His eyes watered from the toxic fumes burning in his lungs.

I'm not going to destroy much of anything, unless I figure a way out of here.

He glanced around the room for a way out of the increasingly inhospitable space. The door he'd entered through had disappeared when he'd removed the disc. And now, the disc was hidden somewhere within the metallic soup of Tiamat's opening sarcophagus. Once the sulfur saturated the air, he'd be as good as dead. And with no source of oxygen, King wasn't sure his regenerative abilities would be able to restore him.

Adding to his dilemma, he couldn't be sure any action he took was his own. The creature had somehow manipulated him into setting aside the spear. Then, completely unaware, he'd been compelled to open the one thing he'd had no intention of opening.

The gas was quickly filling the room. No longer just coming from the containment chamber, King noticed plumes of sulfur shooting out from vents in the ceiling and floor, as well. With few options, he dashed to the nearby wall, grabbed the spear and turned to face the sarcophagus, just as a long, bony arm reached out through the liquefied lid.

The creature inside pulled itself up. Distracted by the sight, King was unaware of a series of hisses behind him, signaling the sudden release of sixteen more stasis tubes. Sixteen black, carapace-covered bodies began to shake with new life as the liquid that had sustained and nourished them for three millennia drained away into the floor.

All King could do between coughs was watch, as a pale, slender form slid from its prison and lifted itself to its full, twelve-foot height. The creature before him was unlike anything he'd ever imagined. Its pale blue skin shimmered in the ambient light, rippling with energy. Its two legs and arms were extraordinarily long and skeletal, giving King the impression of a great insect. But unlike the Girtablilu, the alien was bipedal. Distinctly humanoid. Its head was much larger than its wire-thin neck should have been able to support. Despite its unnatural bodily appearance, it was the face—or lack of a face—that held King's attention. The skeletal structure of the face suggested eye sockets, a nose, a mouth and jaw, but it's 'face' was a sheet of shimmering skin. No eyes. No mouth or nose. For a moment, it seemed impossible, but there were species on Earth that breathed through skin and absorbed nutrients without a mouth, so King could understand how a creature such as this could exist.

The creature was completely nude except for an ornately decorated headdress that adorning its massive head—a headdress that looked very familiar to King. But closer reflection on that would have to wait. As he continued assessing the creature's appearance, he was stunned by a new revelation. The lack of clothing revealed something even more disturbing than anything so far. Its anatomy suggested that it was indeed very much a female. Two round breasts heaved as she stretched. They were positioned relatively in the appropriate anatomical position to any human's breasts, which made her appearance all the more unnerving for him.

NOW I CAN LOOK ON YOU, her thoughts boomed in King's oxygen-deprived mind.

He wasn't sure how she could see him without eyes, but no good would come from him trying to understand her anatomy. He tried to lift the spear to throw at her, but his arms were already far too weak for such an exertion.

I'm going to die. Again.

YES. YOU ARE, she said. *AND AFTERWARDS, THE BOY YOU HAVE SWORN TO PROTECT WILL BE BROUGHT TO ME. I WILL TAKE VENGEANCE ON THE SON OF MARDUK.*

Belshazzar? Unable to speak, King could only think the questions now rapid-firing through his mind. *But why? He's done nothing to you.*

HIS ANCESTOR WAS THE OFFENDER. NIMROD, WHO IMPRISONED ME HERE. IF I CANNOT HAVE MY VENGEANCE ON HIM, I WILL SEE HIS OFFSPRING SUFFER IN HIS STEAD.

I doubt Nimrod will care.

King dropped to his knees in another fit. A spray of crimson spewed from his nose and mouth with each cough. If not for his grip on the shaft of the spear, he would have collapsed completely to the floor.

A sudden cacophony of clicks brought the weakened King's attention behind him. Sixteen Girtablilu now stood around him, watching the exchange with interest. Their multiple insectoid eyes shifted simultaneously between him and their mistress, Tiamat. Other than that, their arachnid-like limbs remained in place. Their saber arms unmoving.

This was supposed to be his army. They were supposed to have assisted him with his mission.

So why aren't you guys doing your thing?

BECAUSE THEY CANNOT. I ALREADY TOLD YOU, THEY CANNOT HELP YOU. Tiamat moved toward him, her movements little more than a glide across the room. With a grace that King would have thought impossible for a creature of her stature, she knelt down and turned her empty face toward his, like she could look at him eye to eye. Gently, she removed the spear from his hand and laid it aside. *THEIR REBELLION WAS VANQUISHED. THEY HAVE SEEN THEIR ERROR AND WILL SERVE THEIR MISTRESS WITHOUT QUESTION. YOU ARE WITHOUT HOPE.*

Tiamat drew closer. She reached a long, slender, three-fingered hand up to his face and stroked it gently. Almost apologetically.

YOU ARE A MOST FASCINATING HUMAN, JACK SIGLER, she whispered in his mind. *YOUR REGENERATIVE CAPABILITIES INTRIGUE ME IN WAYS YOU CANNOT POSSIBLY IMAGINE.*

"I just have one thing to say before I die," he managed to say aloud. Blood bubbled from his lips, dripping down his tunic to pool onto the floor around his knees.

AND WHAT IS THAT?

"I...understand why you...leave the fighting...to the Girtablilu." In one swift motion, King shot up from the floor, pulled the sword he'd taken from the unconscious soldier from his belt, and swung it directly at the creature's head.

The clang of metal echoed throughout the chamber, as Tiamat sprang back from the blow, backhanding King in the process. Her insect-like arms were surprisingly strong, and he flew back into the awaiting arms of a gargantuan Girtablilu.

FOOL! YOU THINK I CAN BE KILLED SO EAS...

The voice in King's spinning brain flickered out before the thought could be completed. The creature staggered back, reaching up to her head in surprise and anger. An arc of electric current shot out from her headdress, striking her extended fingers with a sharp *crack*. She screamed something in a language King couldn't understand and pointed accusingly at him with a skeletal finger.

The Girtablilu stared at her.

She screamed another indecipherable command, but the monsters still didn't budge.

King wheezed for breath as he extricated himself from the scorpion man's razor-sharp arms. The lacerations to his skin were already healing, but he wasn't certain how much longer he could survive in the sulfurous atmosphere. It didn't matter much at this point.

He'd already won.

"You made..." He hacked uncontrollably for a moment, then resumed speaking. "...you made one major mistake, lady. You shouldn't have threatened the kid. It just pissed me off." King looked at the sixteen scorpion creatures that towered over him. "I don't know if you guys can understand me or not." He nodded toward Tiamat's trembling form. "She's all yours."

The Girtablilu glared at their alien mistress, who continued shouting unintelligible commands. Ignoring her, they scuttled slowly forward, raising their mantis-like forearms aggressively as they did. The last things King heard before allowing the darkness to take him were the strange alien screams and the sound of rending flesh.

It was a good way to for King to die.

26

The Ruined City of Eridu, Topside

The battle raged, but Sereb-Meloch couldn't contain his grin as he looked over the blood-soaked battlefield. As sword and spear clashed below him, the heavens roared above. Though it was approaching noon, the sun hid trembling behind a wall of blue-green clouds, casting the land into near darkness. Thunder crashed as streaks of lightning pierced the sand-swept earth like great lances.

My queen's wrath, the high priest reflected. *Her assistance in our time of need. Thank you, my goddess. Praise be to you, Mistress Tiamat.*

Nebuchadnezzar's forces fell like ants beneath his boot. Some even dropped dead without so much as a scratch from an enemy blade. More of Tiamat's might, he supposed. Her powerful reach slew her enemies, even while she was confined in her tomb. Granted, even his own men seemed to be dying inexplicably as well. But they were paid mercenaries. Only loyal to the gold coins that jangled in their purses. They neither knew the wonders of Tiamat nor her true power, which would soon, as a consort to the mighty queen, be his.

"It will not be long now, Your Highness," Sereb-Meloch said to the prince caged beside him. "Soon, your grandfather's army will be little more than drying bones soaked in their own blood, and we will enter the goddess mother's sacred tomb." He turned to glare at Belshazzar. "And you will be handed over to her as the final sacrifice."

The prince scowled at the lanky priest, then spit between the bars. "Achelous will find a way to stop you."

Sereb-Meloch returned his gaze to the bloodbath below and chuckled. "I doubt that. Though I am not certain how he managed to survive our last encounter, my spies reported that he entered the tomb earlier this morning. The goddess predicted as much. It was part of her plan from the beginning. Your protector will have freed her by now, which means, he is already dead."

The priest had already accounted for every possible eventuality. There was nothing the child, or anyone else for that matter, could do that would surprise him.

For now though, he contented himself with watching the carnage ensue. The three hundred warriors that had begun the fight had dwindled down to nearly a hundred and fifty. Namtar and Tiamba had been a most awesome spectacle to behold. Their powerful scorpion tails lashed out madly at their enemies, impaling them before hurling them away like rubbish. Those that their tails didn't kill were dispatched by their blade-like arms, slicing whole men in two with a single swipe.

Beholding their power, Sereb-Meloch found himself thankful once more for finding the strange headdress he now wore within Nimrod's treasure hoard. It had been that single discovery that had set him in motion to his destiny. It was the moment he'd placed the head piece on his brow that the goddess Tiamat had revealed herself to him. She'd waited patiently for over three thousand years for a man such as himself to come to her aid. A man with vision enough to see the putrid stench of the decaying world, who could understand the need for the destruction of the old, so that a new, more glorious world could be established. The fact that she had promised him dominion over the new world had been only a small incentive for what he'd done.

Another blast of lightning lashed out at the great ziggurat's foundation, shaking the earth beneath his feet. For a moment, the fighting ceased and all eyes turned to face the destruction left in the wake of the blast. A giant chunk of ancient temple had been crushed to powder, revealing a strange metal surface underneath.

The Great Sarcophagus.

The high priest's heart hammered in his chest. This was it. His queen would soon reveal herself to the world. He watched in rapt attention as the colorful metal underneath the old stone shimmered and swirled, turning itself into a rippling pool of molten liquid.

"She's coming!" he shouted. No one but the prince could hear him amid the rumble of thunder and tempest of wind that sailed past them, swooping down into the valley.

Finally, after an eternity of waiting, something stepped through the new opening. A long, black, spider-like leg. Then another. And another. He watched as even more extricated themselves from the ancient tomb. One by one, sixteen massive Girtablilu scurried out from the rubble of the fallen temple's stones. Countless tiny black eyes surveyed the stupefied warriors who gawked hopelessly back at them.

"Her honor guard," Sereb-Meloch said. Pride and triumph practically dripped off his tongue with each word. And why shouldn't it? His victory was at hand. His kingdom would reign before the day was finished.

And then, as if a great hammer had been hurled down from the sky to crush his aspirations to dust, the foreigner, Achelous, emerged from the swirling portal. A great spear clutched tightly in one hand and a large, light blue object in the other.

"What has happened? What could this mean?" Sereb-Meloch's voice nearly squeaked.

Belshazzar answered him with contempt, but Sereb-Meloch hadn't heard the prince. He was too busy watching as the unkillable man pointed here and there, sending his army of Girtablilu into the fray. The priest watched in horror as the old man, Daniy'yel, rushed up to Achelous with a great smile, leading two horses along on leads. Then, after a quick embrace with the prophet of Yahweh, Achelous mounted a horse, sat tall upon its back and scanned the terrain. After the briefest of moments, his gaze stopped directly on Sereb-Meloch, who sat astride his own horse, on the top of the ridge. Achelous lifted the round object high into the air.

The thing was featureless, but still recognizable as an oversized, almost feminine... Sereb-Meloch choked when he realized what it was.

It was a head.

The head of his goddess.

Tiamat was dead.

Seeing the high priest's recognition, Achelous's smile broadened. He hurled the decapitated head into the middle of the battlefield, then pointed directly at the high priest.

The meaning was clear: *I'm coming for you.*

A wave of anger shot through Sereb-Meloch's veins like an infusion of magma. How dare the infidel lay hands on the goddess! How dare he discard her sacred head as easily as he would that of a sacrificial bull!

But the foreigner's arrogance would be his undoing. With Nimrod's headdress, Sereb-Meloch could turn Achelous's own army of Girtablilu against him. The same device that had allowed him control of Tiamba and Namtar, would also enslave their brothers as well.

Sereb-Meloch looked on as Achelous, upon his horse, bolted across the valley, sweeping through the field of stupefied warriors, who were now busy defending themselves against the onslaught of scorpion men. The high priest waited patiently, allowing his enemy to draw closer.

Then, believing his timing would be perfect, the high priest released his mental command, trusting the headdress to relay it to the monstrous creatures below. Tiamba and Namtar stopped and turned to seek out Achelous. Their sixteen brothers did the same. Sereb-Meloch could almost see the hunger building in each monster's multitude of eyes, and he held his breath in anticipation of their attack.

But it never came.

Instead, the great beasts swept behind the racing horse and followed the foreigner, as he beelined toward the high priest's position.

Panic building, Sereb-Meloch reissued his command, but the scorpion men ignored it. "Do as I command!" he shouted, but Achelous and the eighteen Girtablilu still charged forward. Now desperate, he sought out Captain Zaidu in an attempt to signal the mercenary regarding his current predicament. But Zaidiu was nowhere in sight. Warriors from both sides could now be seen scurrying away from the carnage of Eridu, fleeing the rampaging horde of scorpion monsters led by a single human champion. Both Nebuchadnezzar's and Sereb-Meloch's own men were running for the hills in all directions, as the thunder boomed angrily overhead.

Out of options, the high priest of the fallen Tiamat wheeled his horse around and followed the example of his mercenaries.

27

The Ruined City of Eridu

King, Belshazzar and Daniel watched as the last of the Girtablilu slipped through the portal and into the subterranean ship. It had taken two weeks to do it, but the creatures, with the help of their human companions, had managed to repair the vessel enough to soon break Earth's orbit. The remaining repairs, however, were best left to those genetically predisposed to such tasks.

"So are you going to tell us now?" Belshazzar asked impatiently, as the liquid metal door to the ship solidified.

"Tell you what?" King asked. He leaned back against a large stone that had once adorned the ziggurat.

"What happened in there," the prince said. "You have been promising to tell me 'later' ever since you pulled me out of that cage."

King glanced at Daniel, who smiled back at him. After several moments, King shrugged. "Sure, why not," he said. "You know that the Girtablilu aren't from this world, right?"

The prince nodded. "Are they from the spirit world?"

King smiled and shook his head. "They're from another world out there," he said, pointing up into the starlit sky. "Probably similar to our own, but with some vast differences." He paused, trying to figure out how best to explain the next bit to someone with no concept of astrophysics or biology. "The Girtablilu had been...um, bred with a specific purpose in mind. They had been enslaved by another race...an empire that traveled to different worlds with the purpose of conquest."

"Like the Assyrians," Belshazzar said.

"Yeah, sort of like the Assyrians. And about three thousand years ago, this empire set their eyes on Earth. But they couldn't breathe our air."

The prince cocked his head inquisitively.

"Just trust me on that, will you?" King said, trying to head the next question off at the pass. "They couldn't breathe our air, so they sent a vessel here that could turn our air into something they could breathe."

"Only it crashed before they could do it."

"Exactly. The ship could change the air, but the Girtablilu, in rebellion of their masters, had sabotaged it so it couldn't fly. When it crashed, it spread its roots into the soil and attempted to proceed with its original mission, but the conversion was stopped before it could do any real damage."

Daniel spoke up at this point. "I have already told you about the rebellion, as well as your ancestor, Nimrod's, part in all this."

The child nodded.

"Well," King went on, "Just as the terraforming—air changing—device's functions were automated—able to work without someone operating it—apparently so was the ship's repair mechanisms. That liquid stuff we saw all over the ship? Those are really tiny, um, creatures. We call them nanobots in my time. Millions of mechanized creatures smaller than insects that constantly build and repair. It took them nearly three thousand years, but apparently they finally got the terraforming functions of the ship back online. They simply needed someone to enter the vessel to start the programming."

"Which you did," the prince said with a wry smile.

"Which I did," King agreed. He went onto describe his encounter with Tiamat and the freeing of her hold on the scorpion men. "After I recovered," he continued, "The Girtablilu shut down both the terraforming apparatus and the mechanism that powered the psychic control unit within Sereb-Meloch's headdress."

"Wait a minute," Belshazzar said. "If the Girtablilu shut down the device that could help them breathe, how is it they seem to breathe our air just fine?"

King smiled at the question. The boy certainly had an analytical brain on his shoulders. "I'm not entirely sure, but I think I figured that out. After working with them these past two weeks, I've had a lot of time to think about how Namtar and Tiamba survived for so long in our world. I was also able to watch and study their physiology more closely, now that they weren't trying to skewer me with their tails." His hand moved to the non-existent scar on his abdomen where he'd been impaled. "Many creatures with exoskeletons—insects, crustaceans, spiders—do not breathe the same way that we do. They pull what they need from the environment around them through pores. Both alien species breathed this way, and I think it helps them survive in harsh environments."

"There is something *I* am curious about," Daniel said finally. "The Girtablilu treated you with such reverence. Such high regard. You said yourself that they knew the name you bore in your previous life. Did you ever discover why this is?"

King shook his head. "No idea. As you know, they are incapable of speaking, in the traditional sense. Just emotions and body language, as well as a primitive mental communication. They weren't really able to answer any of my questions. The things I've just told you are pretty much pure speculation on my part." He thought about the Girtablilu's respect and admiration for him and he smiled. "I'll probably never know." Though, given his experience with time travel, he suspected his future self would likely discover the truth at some point.

The three sat in their camp, looking up at the stars for several long minutes. The air was warm, but not as fetid as it had been when King first arrived in Eridu. The damage done to the environment by the ship would take some time to heal, and so the temperature would remain slightly cooler than normal. King decided he could live with that.

Belshazzar broke the silence. "So what happens next?"

"Well, I imagine they'll have the ship fully operational in a month or so," King said. "Since the excavation of this place around my time didn't reveal a huge spacecraft buried underneath, I'm willing to bet they'll take off and head somewhere to enjoy their freedom."

"No, not that," the prince said. "I mean about us. About you? And about the heretic?"

King smiled. "I imagine Sereb-Meloch will be taken care of soon enough," he said. "As for you, you'll be heading back to Babylon with Daniel. Now that the threat is over, there is no reason for your grandfather to either kill you or use you to unseal the tomb." He stood up, moved over to a large chest left by a general in

Nebuchadnezzar's army, and opened it. Reaching in, he pulled out a large piece of sackcloth containing Tiamat's severed head. "Take this back to him. And tell him the man who did this to a goddess is watching over you. He tries to harm you in any way, this will be a reminder of what waits for him. You got that?"

The boy's nose crinkled at the decaying smell already wafting from the cadaverous head. But he nodded slowly. "You'll not come with us?"

King shook his head. "Best I don't," he said, picking up some of his gear and walking over to his horse. He began packing the horse down with everything he would need and looked back at the boy. "My life is...complicated." *And dangerous to mortals.* He walked over to the prince and placed a hand gently on the boy's shoulder. "But I'll check on you. I promise."

Belshazzar, fighting back tears, slung his arms around King's waist and hugged him with all his might. After a while, he released his grip and dashed away, out of sight. After watching the boy go, Daniel strode up to King with a smile.

"Well done, my friend," he said, holding out his hand.

King accepted the hand and shook.

"All right, old man," King said. "Now it's your turn. Before I left for Eridu, you mentioned you had something else to tell me, when this was all over. Let's hear it."

Daniel smiled up at him and chuckled. "Oh, that," he said. "I was given a very specific message for you in a dream. Your betrothed and your daughter will both be well looked after until your return. You have nothing to fear. They are safely in his care."

The news, coming from this man known the world over for his incredibly accurate predictions and wisdom, was almost more than King could bear. In over two hundred years, there had not been a day that went by where he hadn't thought of Sara and Fiona in some way, praying to a god he hadn't entirely been sure existed, that they would be cared for. That they would be watched over. And here the prophet Daniel was telling him in no uncertain terms...his prayers had been heard and answered. More than that, if he read between the lines, Daniel was telling him he would make it back to them, in which case, he'd be the one doing the watching over.

Smiling, he embraced the old man, then mounted his horse with a bit more of a spring in his step than before this adventure had started. As he spurred the horse forward and headed out into the desert, he entertained only a single thought: he had many years ahead of him before he would see them again, but knowing they would be safe until that time meant everything in the world to him.

28

**The Fertile Crescent, 75 Miles West of Eridu
Eleven Months Later**

Sereb-Meloch couldn't stop shaking from within the pitch blackness of the cave. It had been nearly a year since the debacle at Eridu. Yet, he couldn't stop looking over his shoulder. Couldn't stop imagining every sound—every drop of water falling from a stalactite—was the sound of stealthy footsteps coming for him.

If you do this, Sereb-Meloch relived the words Achelous had uttered, as Zaidu had prepared to remove the man's head. *I swear to the one and only God that matters... I will make you suffer more than you ever imagined possible.*

And somehow, the man had actually survived decapitation and purifying fires. No mortal man could survive such destruction.

Achelous is not a man, Sereb-Meloch thought. *Perhaps he is Enki. Or Enlil.* He shuddered at his next guess. *Or perhaps my soldiers were correct in speculating the foreigner to be the earthly incarnation of Marduk himself?*

After all, Marduk had defeated his goddess once before. No one else could have been capable of such a feat. Certainly no mortal.

Achelous's own words gave a clue as to his true identity. *I swear to the one and only God that matters*, he had said. He spoke of Marduk, hadn't he? He was the greatest of all the gods, after all. Everyone, other than the deluded Hebrews, knew the truth of that.

A sudden rush of dread swept through the priest's limbs, as he huddled over the abysmal fire he'd managed to strike up in the safety of his cavern. He'd angered the king of the gods. He'd earned Marduk's wrath. Surely there was nowhere on Earth that he could hide from such a being.

And yet, he remained sequestered deep in the bowels of the mountains, living on the blind fish, insects and snails he managed to scavenge in the cave. He dared go out only at night and even then, for short treks in search of wood and other supplies he might need during the day. He'd become a bedraggled excuse for a man, a beggar whose cup was filled only by the natural world around him.

He threw the last remaining piece of wood on the fire and shivered. "What could be a worse torture than what I did to Achelous?" he mumbled, remembering the threat all over again. What horrible fate awaited him, if this god-who-resembled-a-man ever found him?

A strained giggle slipped unbidden past his lips.

What fate? What fate? What fate? he repeated in his thoughts.

The giggle intensified as he plucked a squirming slug from the fire and slid it into his mouth.

What will he do to me when he catches me?
What fate?

What fate?

The giggle avalanched into a deep throated fit of laughter. Sereb-Meloch knew he should be quieter. He might attract the attention of the gods. But he couldn't help himself. Achelous's words to him just before the axe had fallen across the man-god's neck just wouldn't go away.

I will make you suffer more than you ever imagined possible.

"Sereb-Meloch..."

The priest flinched, spinning around.

He was still alone.

A warbling shadow darted across the wall, tearing a scream from his lips.

"Behind you," came a whispering voice.

He spun and found no one.

A tug on his head made him yelp and turn back in time to see a clean cut clump of his hair float down into the fire and curl in on itself.

"Achelous!" the priest shouted. "Finish this!" He knew his mind was faltering and longed for release, but he lacked the bravery to end his own life.

The tick of a rock falling turned him to the left.

The shadows moved.

The priest stood on shaking legs and walked toward the darkness. "Achelous! Take me now!"

Silence.

The shadows remained still.

He stood there for minutes, peering into the darkness.

Two eyes suddenly appeared, no more than two feet away. "Boo."

Then they were gone, and as Sereb-Meloch screamed and screamed, his voice was joined by the laughter of a man who could not die. The priest fell to the ground, thrashing and wailing, knowing that his torment had only just begun.

AFTERWORD

Imagine, if you will, that George Lucas (or now, perhaps Mickey Mouse) knocked on your door and asked you to not only co-star in the next Star Wars movie, but also to have carte blanche to play in the creative sandbox and help develop the new direction his universe was going to take. Yeah, that's kind of how I felt when Jeremy approached me about participating in the very first *Jack Sigler Continuum* book.

You see, although I'm an author, I've been a fan of Jeremy's stuff from the beginning. It was he, in fact, that inspired me to throw off the shackles of my own fears, forget about 'dreaming' about being a writer, and actually pursue my passion full force. After all, he's come an amazingly long way since his humble beginnings self-publishing at Lulu.com (incidentally, the first place I started as well).

The point is, like so many of you, I've been a fan of Jack Sigler since I first read *Pulse*. I've followed his and the Chess Team's adventures from day one, and I loved them. I thrilled at the other co-authored novellas, loving every word of them and never dreaming that one day, I might be chosen to be counted among them.

Then, one day, it happened. I got that e-mail. Jeremy graciously asked me if I'd be interested in co-authoring the first book of a new Jack Sigler series. Needless to say, I didn't hesitate.

But here's the most amazing part. It's something that many of you might not know about Jeremy. Keep in mind, this is his world. His universe. His creation. His baby. If roles were reversed, I'd be the most ridiculously overprotective 'parent' in the world. I'd hover over the co-author, eyeing each word they typed suspiciously. I'd correct. I'd rebuke. I'd reign in any crazy notions the co-author might be considering, for fear that they were about to screw up my universe royally. Well, I have news for you. Jeremy is nothing like that. He was so gracious. So patient. And most importantly, he allowed me absolute freedom to play in his sandbox, however I saw fit. As a matter of fact, as I wrote my portion of this story, he asked me not to tell him anything about what I was doing. He wanted it to be a surprise. Wanted to enjoy the story much the same way as readers would. He allowed me unimaginable freedom to dabble...to torture King and to shape the direction the *Jack Sigler Continuum* series would take. Let me tell you, as a creative person, this is as mighty a feat as anything Jack Sigler could ever do. The trust he has in his co-authors is truly magnificent and unprecedented. But you know what? I think he knows it will pay off in the end...this trust.

So when you think about Jeremy Robinson, the author, you should also think of Jeremy Robinson, the amazing man. Of all the more influential authors I've met during my time as a writer, I can honestly say he's one of the most humble...most sincere...and most down to earth guys you'll ever get to know. And you know what else? He truly cares about you—his fans and his readers. He sees his mission as simple and straight forward: Make you smile. Make you thrill. Make you feel entertained and satisfied. That's just the kind of guy he is.

—J. Kent Holloway
March 25, 2014

ABOUT THE AUTHORS

Jeremy Robinson is the bestselling author of more than forty novels and novellas, including *Island 731*, *SecondWorld*, and the Jack Sigler thriller series, including *Prime*, *Pulse*, *Instinct*, *Threshold*, *Ragnarok* and *Omega*. Robinson is also known as the bestselling horror writer, Jeremy Bishop, author of *The Sentinel*, *The Raven*, the controversial novel, *Torment* and the popular serial novel *Refuge*. His novels have been translated into eleven languages. He lives in New Hampshire with his wife and three children.

Visit him online at www.jeremyrobinsononline.com.

J. Kent Holloway is the author of six edge-of-your-seat paranormal thrillers and mysteries. A real-life paranormal investigator and 'Legend Tripper,' he explores the realms of myth, folklore and the unknown, in the southeast United States in his spare time. When not writing or scouring the globe for ghosts, cryptids and all manner of legends, he works as a forensic death investigator.

Visit him online at kenthollowayonline.com.

COMING IN 2014
FROM JEREMY ROBINSON

JACK SIGLER rejoins CHESS TEAM for the next full-length adventure in *SAVAGE*.

A guidebook to the Jack Sigler / Chess Team universe, *ENDGAME*, will be a handy reference for the team's past missions, with some hints at what's coming next!

ALSO AVAILABLE
BY J. KENT HOLLOWAY

THE DARK HOLLOWS...

Something sinister has awakened in a mysterious, dead patch of land in the foothills of the Appalachians...an evil that has been there long before the white man explored the primeval hills. And it has a hunger that must be sated.

Only one cursed man has the skill and knowledge to stop it. But to the people of Boone Creek, the enigmatic Ezekiel Crane might just be worse than the creature he's hell-bent on destroying.

Available at Amazon, BN.com, and wherever books are sold.

Lightning Source UK Ltd.
Milton Keynes UK
UKOW02f0051020916

282047UK00005B/192/P